JC N.D. CMH
CS M.G. LSW
HTW JAP

ADAM'S BRIDE

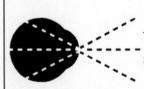

This Large Print Book carries the
Seal of Approval of N.A.V.H.

ADAM'S BRIDE

AN OLD-FASHIONED ROMANCE BLOOMS IN THE HEART OF NEW ENGLAND

LISA HARRIS

THORNDIKE PRESS
A part of Gale, Cengage Learning

GALE
CENGAGE Learning

Detroit • New York • San Francisco • New Haven, Conn • Waterville, Maine • London

GALE
CENGAGE Learning™

LIBRARY OF CONGRESS CATALOGING-IN-PUBLICATION DATA

Harris, Lisa, 1969–
  Adam's bride : an old-fashioned romance blooms in the heart of New England / by Lisa Harris. — Large print ed.
    p. cm. — (Thorndike Press large print Christian fiction)
  (Massachuetts brides ; bk.3)
    ISBN-13: 978-1-4104-2748-9
    ISBN-10: 1-4104-2748-X
    1. Large type books. I. Title.
PS3608.A78315A33 2010
813'.6—dc22   2010014471

Published in 2010 by arrangement with Barbour Publishing, Inc.

Printed in Mexico
1 2 3 4 5 6 7 14 13 12 11 10

Dear Reader,

From the windswept Boston seacoast to the lush Connecticut Valley, Massachusetts, in the late 1800s is a place of unparalleled beauty and rich history. Writing these stories about Michaela, Rebecca, and Adam was like taking a step back into history for me and one I thoroughly enjoyed. It also was a journey of self-discovery for my own life. As my characters struggled to face life's challenges of loss, forgiveness, and finding God's will, I found myself learning spiritual lessons alongside them. What a wonderful reminder that in the midst of life's conflicts, faith can be renewed and love worth keeping found.

My prayer for each of you is that you might discover the freedom of following God with all your heart and that you might lean on Him no matter what circumstances you are facing right now. He is faithful.

Stop by my Web site at www.lisaharris writes.com. I'd love to hear from you.

Blessings,
Lisa Harris

The steps of a good man are ordered by the LORD: and he delighteth in his way. Though he fall, he shall not be utterly cast down: for the LORD upholdeth him with this hand.

Psalm 37:23–24

ONE

Cranton, Massachusetts, 1886

A cold February wind ripped through Adam Johnson's coat as he hurried down one of Cranton's wooden sidewalks. The crunch of snow beneath his heavy boots brought a smile to his lips. Instinctively, he checked the direction of the wind with the tip of his finger. He was pleased with the strong westward direction that would ensure a good run of sap from his sugar maple grove.

While the majority of the townspeople huddled in front of their fireplaces, he had no complaints about the frosty weather. An early spring meant disaster for him, because without a hard freeze at night his syrup would take on a leathery taste, something he couldn't afford with this year's crop.

Jingling the bag of nails in the palm of his hand, he whistled a nameless tune he'd heard his father sing a hundred times. Last year Adam harvested thirty gallons of syrup.

This year he planned on setting out five hundred buckets for an even bigger yield.

A boy whose back was hunched against the wind bumped into him as he walked. Adam struggled to keep his footing on the icy path. His bag of nails hit the ground and scattered across the boardwalk as he watched a scrawny boy take off with his wallet.

"Hey!" He lunged for the kid, but the wiry figure slipped from his grasp.

The guttersnipe was fast, but Adam was faster. Months of hard work on his farm had turned his boyish stature into that of a man. In contrast, the thin youth in front of him looked as if he could use a good hot meal. At the edge of the alleyway beside the First Bank of Cranton, Adam gripped the boy's collar and held on tight.

"I believe you have something of mine."

"Please, Mister . . ." The boy threw the wallet onto the ground, then slithered out of Adam's grasp, leaving his threadbare coat behind.

Immigrants.

Irish, Poles, and Italians had poured into the area, bringing crime with them. Granted, he'd heard of the horrid conditions many of these foreigners had escaped from in Eastern Europe. Those who hadn't settled in the big cities like Boston and New York had made their way across the eastern states to find work in the dozens of mills where life was strenuous, but at least they had food to eat and a bed to sleep in at night.

Regardless of how much compassion a God-fearing man like himself ought to feel toward these people, his brother had been murdered in cold blood by one of the immigrants. That was something he could never forget — or forgive.

Adam snatched up his wallet and opened the soft leather pouch. Empty. How that cavorting thief had managed to clean him out in such a short time, he had no idea, but he wouldn't let this go. Something had to be done. He crossed the street with broad, determined steps in search of the sheriff. The wooden door of the jailhouse slammed against the inside brick wall as Adam stormed into the office.

"Sheriff Briggs, I've got a complaint to lodge."

"Get in line." The balding lawman waved a pudgy hand at a chair. "You're the third person this morning who's come in here unhappy about something."

"Why are you still sitting here?"

"I didn't want to miss listening to your

11

rambling complaints." The sheriff scowled from behind his desk. "How much money did the boy take from you?"

Adam gripped the back of the offered chair with his hands. "How'd you know I was robbed?"

The sheriff's jowls jiggled as he laughed. "Like I said, you're not the first person to come here in a rage."

Adam didn't see the humor in the situation. "The young ruffian stole five dollars, and that's not including the bag of nails that he scattered across the boardwalk."

"Wilton Hunter lost seventy-five dollars."

Adam stepped around the chair and slammed his palms against the top of the sheriff's desk. "So what are you going to do about it?"

"The boys' names are Edward Malik and —"

"He's Polish," Adam interrupted, feeling the tension in his jaw tighten. "I've said before, if we don't do something about the number of —"

"I said *boys*. Plural, meaning there's more than one. We're pretty sure the second is Simon Miller's boy."

"Figures." Miller was a well-respected member of the Cranton community. Adam had never heard of any problems with the storekeeper's youngest son, but spending too much time with the wrong crowd could easily change that. "Doesn't the Good Book say that bad company corrupts good morals?"

"So you're automatically assuming that Edward Malik's to blame?"

"A Pole murdered my brother, Sheriff. Why would this one be any different?" Adam turned toward the wanted posters and ripped the familiar sketch off the wall before tossing it down in front of the sheriff. "What other proof do you need?"

"One bad egg shot your brother, Adam. It was a tragic event, but don't let the past cloud your judgment toward an entire group of people. You'd see that we have some fine immigrant families in the area if you could get beyond what happened."

"You weren't there, Sheriff. You didn't see the look of hate in this boy's eyes." Adam jabbed his finger at the poster. "Samuel might have thrown the first punch, but he didn't deserve to be shot down."

"Samuel's death hit us all extremely hard." The sheriff scratched his bald scalp. "But nothing you or I can do will ever bring him back. Don't let one man's foolish actions leave you with a lifetime of bitterness, son."

Adam didn't want the advice, and he sure wasn't through with their conversation. "Why haven't you found his killer yet?"

"Bounty hunters are still looking for him, but we aren't even sure who the murderer is. All we have is a first name and a sketch based on your description."

Adam slammed his fists against the desk. "It's been seventeen months, and you don't even know the killer's last name!"

Was it so wrong for him to want justice for his brother's death? His family seemed to have accepted what happened, but he couldn't. Not when he knew there was a lunatic on the loose who might kill again. Adam had considered taking the law into his own hands. The only thing stopping him was a promise to his sister, Rebecca. He'd never been one to take his promises lightly.

"You know I'll contact you as soon as we get another lead," the sheriff said. The front legs of the sheriff's chair hit the floor with a thud. "As for the thieves, my deputy's out looking for them right now. I'll let you know when we've brought them in."

Five minutes later Adam set out in his buckboard down the snow-covered lane toward his farm. He tried to erase the last vivid image of his dying brother. He loved all six of his brothers and sisters, including little Anna, who had been adopted into his family, but Samuel had also been his best friend. They'd spent countless lazy summer mornings fishing for bass along the Connecticut River, afternoons playing ball or pulling pranks on their other siblings. Besides the fun they'd had together, it had been Samuel who helped him get through his first maple syrup harvest.

His brother had wanted to go to Boston to study to become a doctor but had decided to stay in favor of experimenting with more efficient ways of planting and producing higher yields for the farmers in the area. Together, he and Adam had devoured copies of the Orange Judd's *American Agriculturist* for information on scientific farming while developing their own ideas in the agricultural arena.

One malice-driven bullet waylaid those dreams forever.

A deafening shriek brought Adam out of his bittersweet memories. A grungy mutt at the base of a tree growled at whatever — or whomever — he had cornered in its branches . . . or whoever. Adam glanced up and saw a patch of dark blue fabric peeking through the thick tree. Something wasn't right. Picking his rifle up off the buckboard, he reined the horses a safe distance from

15

the dog, then stepped onto the frosty ground.

The dog turned toward him, ignoring for the moment his treed prey. He growled, showing his teeth. Adam took a step forward, shouting at the dog to get away, but even his animated gestures didn't scare the mutt. Taking aim at the dog, he inched across the snow. Regarding the animal out of the corner of his eye, he squinted against the midday sun to see who was in the tree. Probably some boy playing hooky from school and looking for a bit of adventure. The victim sat precariously on one of the lower branches, partially hidden from view by the thick growth, but far enough up that the vicious dog couldn't get him.

"Watch out! I think he's rabid."

Adam froze at the sound of the female voice coming from the tree. He'd never seen a lady suspended that high up on the branches of a tree. How had she managed to climb so high in a dress?

The dog growled, and Adam turned his attention back to the snarling creature. A dog in such a state was dangerous. If it attacked a person, the consequences could be fatal. And if she'd been bitten . . .

The dog, drooling at the mouth, shifted its gaze back and forth between him and his prey and bared its teeth at Adam, convincing him of the woman's diagnosis of rabies. "I'm going to have to shoot the dog; then I'll help you down."

Taking aim, he pulled the trigger and cringed as his shot echoed across the valley, signaling the end to his grim deed. He felt sorry for the beast, especially if it had been some boy's best friend. But one didn't take chances with rabid animals.

"Name's Adam Johnson," he said, stepping over the motionless animal and moving toward the base of the tree to get a better look at the dog's intended victim.

"I'm Lidia."

"Are you hurt?"

"No, just scared half out of my mind."

Adam rested his hand against the rough bark and looked up into the darkest pair of mahogany eyes he'd ever seen. Her long, auburn hair was pulled back neatly, with one tendril having escaped during the ordeal. Fair skin, rosy cheeks from the winter chill, and her petite stature reminded him of a fairy straight out of a storybook.

A clump of snow fell from the branch and hit him in the nose, knocking some sense back into him. He shook his head and laughed.

"I'm sorry —" she said.

"Not your fault at all, ma'am. Can I help you down?"

With Adam's arms around her waist, Lidia slid onto the ground and tried to catch her breath. After a moment he let go, but she could still feel the warmth of his hands through her thin coat.

Frankly, she found the entire situation utterly ridiculous and certainly embarrassing. Being chased up a tree by a rabid dog was no proper situation for a lady to find herself in, let alone a suitable backdrop for a romantic encounter with a well-built hero. Not that she expected such a silly event to occur. Things like that only happened between the pages of a dime novel or in her imagination.

Her grandmother, her sweet *babcia,* had first planted such wistful yet foolish notions in her head. While she remembered little about the country she left when she was six, she'd never forget memories of cold nights cuddled up with her babcia under a thick quilt, listening to her enchanted stories. But true romantic champions were saved for legends like Lajkonik, the renowned horseman who rode into Kraków to warn the citizens of the impending Tartar raids, or other such tales of bravery her people had

18

passed down for centuries. But she was an American now, she reminded herself. If she was going to make it in this new land she had to put aside such outlandish ideas.

"Can I take you somewhere?"

Lidia jerked her head up at Adam's question. His hair was as black as coal, and his eyes, while dark, had glints of gold in their depths. She'd never been as scared as she had the few moments before he'd arrived. While the rabid dog chased her across the frozen terrain, she'd been quite certain her short life was over. If it hadn't been for a small flock of birds that distracted the aggressive beast, she wouldn't have had the time to make it up the tree.

Then he'd come along.

"You want to take me somewhere?" Lidia glanced at the motionless form of the dog and tried to clear her head. "No. I'm fine, really, and I doubt I'll run into a rabid animal twice in one day. Besides, I'm not going far."

"If you're sure . . ."

She nodded and despite the frigid wind, she felt a warm blush creep up her cheeks. There was something about him that made her want to stop and take a second look. But he must think her to be the most unconventional lady, or perhaps not a lady at all, for hoisting herself up in a tree — no matter what the circumstances.

Quickly saying good-bye, she shoved her hands into the pockets of her threadbare coat and hurried down the icy lane toward the mill, determined to forget this Adam Johnson. She still had a full day's work ahead of her, and there was certainly no time in her life to fantasize about handsome heroes and their legendary conquests. Not when she had a brother to take care of. No. Thankfully, she'd more than likely never see her gallant rescuer again.

Adam reached down to pick up the gun he'd propped against the side of the tree and tried to shake the strange feeling that had swept over him when he'd looked at Lidia. Of course, he was imagining things. Just because it had been months since he'd seen anyone quite as lovely as her was no reason to let his mind wander. Teasing from his older sister, Rebecca, didn't help, either. She might have run off to Boston and snagged herself a husband, but that didn't mean Adam was looking to settle down.

A flash of color in the snow caught his eyes. He bent for a closer look. After sweeping away a layer of powdery snow, he picked up a small Bible with gold lettering on the cover. He opened it to the front page and felt his heart plummet. He hadn't noticed her accent, but the name was evidence enough. Inside the front cover in neat script, was the name Lidia Kowalski. The truth struck him like a second bullet to his brother's heart. The beautiful girl he'd just rescued was Polish.

TWO

"You never told me what Lidia's like."

Adam leaned back in one of the hotel dining room chairs and frowned at Rebecca's pointed statement. "I didn't tell you, because I don't know. I only spoke to her briefly, then offered to take her home. When she refused, I left. That was all."

He pulled off his thick wool gloves then laid them beside his hat on the restaurant table. Normally it was Sarah, his younger sister, who was full of nosy questions, but lately Rebecca had become just as probing. He hadn't planned for anyone to discover that he'd rescued the young woman. If it hadn't been for Rebecca noticing the small, gold-lettered Bible in his coat pocket after church on Sunday, no one would have ever found out. That was when all his troubles began.

Instead of forgetting the incident as he'd wanted, he'd suddenly become some heroic champion ripped straight from the pages of one of those dime novels Rebecca read when she thought no one was looking. And Sarah also found it terribly romantic because he'd "rescued a beautiful maiden in distress," as she'd exclaimed more than once during the past week.

The waitress brought their hot drinks, giving him a reprieve from answering more of Rebecca's questions. He busied himself with adding three teaspoons of sugar to the steaming coffee, then settled back in the wooden chair to take a sip. With the bright yellow and orange flames crackling in the large stone fireplace beside them, it was easy to forget how quickly the temperature was dropping outside. If the cold spell lasted another week or two with its hard freezes at night and temperatures warming up during the days, the conditions for harvesting the sap from his maple trees would be perfect.

"You're telling me that you didn't notice anything about her?" his sister persisted.

Adam groaned inwardly. He hadn't planned to stay in town long today, but Rebecca had convinced him to join her for a cup of coffee at the hotel. While he normally enjoyed spending time with her, he wasn't so sure it had been a good idea with her mind obviously on matchmaking.

Trying to stifle a sneeze, he frowned. "I thought you promised not to bring up a subject even remotely related to matchmaking again."

He took another sip of his coffee and watched his sister out of the corner of his eye. Rebecca's marriage to Luke Hutton last fall had reaffirmed her belief in true love and made her a staunch believer in the institution of marriage. Her efforts to find the same marital bliss for her brother were . . . well . . . in a word, annoying. And it wasn't the first time one of the female members of his family had taken it upon themselves to set him up with someone.

It wasn't as if he didn't love his family, or that he was in any way opposed to the idea of marriage, but at the present he viewed the issue as personal. When it was God's timing to marry he had no doubts that he'd know it and act upon it. So far, he hadn't found the person he intended to spend the rest of his life with. And until then, he was content to wait.

"It was just an innocent question." Rebecca tasted her drink, then added another dash of milk. "You are considered one of the most eligible bachelors in town by most of the single women, and you saved someone's life, so . . . I'm interested."

Adam knew his sister well enough to know that her questions ran far deeper than simple curiosity. He was quite certain that if he'd rescued his neighbor's plump and prim daughter, who was well past the age of marrying, the subject would not have been worthy of resurrecting again.

He strummed his fingers against the table. "She's beautiful — is that what you want me to say?"

"That's a good start." Rebecca leaned forward, a calculated smile on her lips. "What else?"

He squirmed under her scrutiny. How could he admit that he'd dreamed about Lidia every night for the past week? That he'd seen her face every time he closed his eyes. Those soft brown eyes framed with long lashes . . . creamy white skin . . . captivating smile . . .

Then he would remember she was Polish, and his foolish daydreams would vanish. That was something he could never forget. It was why he intended to forget her.

He shoved his hands into his coat pocket, only to be reminded of her Bible that he'd been carrying with him all week. "Her last name is Kowalski."

"I know. I saw it on the Bible."

"She's Polish." He hated the way his

25

clipped words sounded, but that didn't take away the truth — Samuel had been killed by a Pole. Rebecca hadn't seen the vacant look in their brother's eyes as Adam had held him, his chest covered with blood —

"Adam?"

"I know what you're thinking." His stomach clenched at the memories. "Why can't I get over Samuel's death? Why can't I forgive those involved? You weren't there, Rebecca. You didn't watch him take his last breath."

His sister's eyes reflected his own pain. "We all miss Samuel, but Lidia's not responsible for his death. She wasn't the one who took his life. If he'd been named Rudolpho or Tazio would you hate all Italians?"

The muscles in his jaw tensed. "That's not fair. It's not that simple —"

"Sure it is." The intensity in her voice increased. "You've let your hatred for one man spread to an entire nationality."

He shook his head and let his hands coil into tight fists as a searing rage rippled through him. "You just don't get it, do you?"

"I want to understand. We all do."

Why was it that when this vein of conversation erupted he always ended up being the bad guy?

Adam worked to relax his muscles but found it impossible. "You don't know how many times I've begged God to take away this anger that burns inside me, but I'll never forget what happened."

And that I never stopped it.

The thought was sobering. None of them had this mountain of guilt to carry the rest of their lives. He closed his eyes, trying to erase the scene he knew would be forever imprinted on his mind. It had all happened so fast that he hadn't even seen it coming. He hadn't seen the gun until it was too late and Samuel lay dying in a pool of his own blood.

Adam wrapped his fingers around the smooth cover of the Bible and drew it out of his pocket. "I'm not sure what to do with this."

"Don't you plan to return it?"

"I don't know where she lives." He had a dozen excuses ready to throw at her. He had too much work to do at the farm, and the weather was getting worse. . . .

"It can't be too complicated to find her, Adam. After all, Cranton isn't Boston." Rebecca's eyes lit up, and he could see an idea formulating in his sister's mind. "She was walking from town which means she can't live very far away. Maybe she lives on one of the nearby farms."

Rebecca sounded like a detective out to

solve a mystery. She had definitely been reading too many of those dime novels. Life was different. It didn't always have a simple storyline that neatly wrapped up at the end of the book. Look at Samuel. Sometimes things went wrong in real life that would never turn into a happy ending.

Clearing his throat, Adam glanced at his pocket watch. He needed to get back to his farm before dark. "Can I take you home?"

"Thanks, but I'll wait here for Luke." Her brow puckered when he changed the subject, but thankfully she seemed ready to leave it alone. "He's planning to meet me here in about twenty minutes." She leaned across the table and took his hand. "I'm glad I ran into you. With you not living at home anymore, I don't see you nearly enough when I'm back for a visit."

"You're the one who moved to Boston."

She squeezed his hand. "Thankfully, Luke's willing to bring me home once or twice a year."

"That's not enough." Despite her constant prying, he still missed her when she was gone. He laid a few coins on the table to cover the drinks, then leaned over and kissed her on the cheek.

"I'll see you Friday night?"

It had become tradition for the family to

get together on Friday nights. And the family was growing. His father had married Michaela, Rebecca married Luke, and before long, no doubt, there would be other spouses and grandchildren.

Adam picked his hat and gloves up off the table. "Promise not to bring up the subject of Lidia or any other female you think might make the perfect match for me?"

"We just want you to be happy, Adam."

"Promise?"

"I promise."

He couldn't help but smile at her insistence. It felt good to be cared about. "I'll see you Friday night."

Adam said good-bye then stepped out into the cold wind, thankful for the warmth of his coat and heavy gloves. Snow began to fall, the thick flakes covering the icy ground with a white blanket. His sister was right about letting go, and he knew it. But knowing what was right and actually doing it were simply not the same thing.

Sneezing twice, he tried to ignore the growing ache that was beginning to spread across his body. He didn't have time to be sick. Tapping his sugar maples was going to take every ounce of energy he had. He could ask for help from his father and his younger brother Mark, but this was something he wanted to do on his own. To prove to himself that he was capable of running this farm.

The silhouette of a familiar figure yanked him out of his thoughts. He stopped abruptly in front of the sheriff's office and stared at the young woman leaving the mercantile. The hem of her dark blue dress fluttered in the wind beneath her threadbare coat as she hugged a thick package to her chest. Even before she turned, he knew for certain it was Lidia. He wasn't sure how, but he'd memorized every detail of her face after their one brief encounter. The slight lilt in each step and the way her smile lit up her face. He'd seen her over and over in his dreams at night, but today he was awake and this was real.

Her gaze met his, and she narrowed the distance between them until she was standing in front of him. "Mr. Johnson, how good it is to see you again."

"Please, you can . . . you can call me Adam." He didn't get tongue-tied in front of women. It had to be all the nonsense of Rebecca's matchmaking attempts. Lidia didn't affect him that way. She couldn't. She was Polish.

"I was hoping to run into you again." Holding the package with one hand, Lidia pushed back a long strand of dark hair the crisp wind had blown into her eyes. "I wanted to thank you again for coming to my rescue."

"It was nothing, really." He kept his sentences brief, determined not to notice her wide brown eyes or the sweet curve of her smile. "Nothing any decent person wouldn't have done for someone else."

She frowned, and he wondered what he'd said to take away the sparkle in her eyes. Just because he was attempting to keep his distance from her didn't mean he had wanted to be rude. Besides the fact that they were strangers, what he'd said was true. Any decent man, or woman for that matter, would have done exactly the same.

He pulled her Bible out of his pocket. "I almost forgot. You dropped this in the snow. I discovered it after you'd left, and I didn't know where to find you."

He handed her the book, feeling like an awkward schoolboy. A part of him had wanted to find her again, but now that she was here, he felt as if his emotions were piled in a jumbled heap around him. If only he could see her in a different light. If only being Polish didn't matter to him.

"I can't thank you enough." Her smile broadened as she took the book. "It was a gift from my parents. I thought I'd never see it again. I guess I'm doubly indebted to you now."

"It was nothing, really." Adam fidgeted, not knowing what to say. Maybe there was nothing else that needed to be said.

"All the same, I do appreciate it."

He tipped his hat and took an awkward step back. "I'm on my way home, so if you'll excuse me."

Lidia nodded solemnly, her stomach churning as she continued toward the outskirts of town. Fingering the smooth cover of her Bible that she'd stuffed inside the pocket of her coat, she felt tears well up in her eyes. She wiped them away with the back of her hand and took a deep breath, determined to control her spiraling emotions. She'd been a fool to let herself daydream about the handsome stranger who'd rescued her from that rabid mutt. Adam Johnson had been right. He'd done nothing more than any other person in the same circumstance would have done. She foolishly misread the looks of attraction in his eyes as he'd helped her down from the tree.

The fact was he was no different than any other man she'd met. Either they wanted her for affections she'd never give a man until she was properly married, or they wanted nothing to do with her because of her heritage. The same was true with most of the women. Both the well-to-do immigrants and the Yankees looked down at girls like her who were forced to work because of their financial situation. She'd seen the same condescension reflected in Adam's eyes. It was a look that made her feel like a second-class citizen. As if being Polish meant that she wasn't a true American. But she *was* American — she would show everyone that Poland was nothing more than a distant memory to her. A story like her babcia's stories. Nothing more.

Pulling her coat closer around her, she shivered against the icy wind. For years, she'd worked to ensure that she never spoke with an accent. She strived to demonstrate the refined characteristics of a lady. Her hard work had paid off — she'd made a few friends who hadn't noticed how different she was. Life had become almost normal. Then her parents' death a year ago changed all of that. No longer was there time for fancy frivolities like tea parties with her friends and picnics on lazy Sunday afternoons. She had to support not only herself but her brother, as well, and the only time she was allowed to escape the confines of the mill was for church or when her boss, Mrs. Moore, sent her to town on an errand.

Hurrying through the snow, Lidia let the tears run freely. Her brother had just turned thirteen. God hadn't meant for a boy his age to be raised by his older sister who had yet to turn twenty. He needed a mother to love him and a father to teach him the Word of God and how to act like a man — something she could never do for him.

Sometimes it's just so hard, God.

She tried to swallow the lump of pain in her throat. When she'd met Adam Johnson, something about him had reminded her of all she yearned for in life. Foolish notions of falling in love and living happily ever after were not luxuries she normally allowed herself to indulge in. They were nothing more than silly dreams of being rescued from the life she was trapped in. That would never happen to her.

Instead, she would spend her days working long hours at the mill. Every spare moment was used reading from the Bible or works of poetry such as N. P. Willis and John Greenleaf Whittier, graciously lent to her by dear Mrs. Gorski from church. If she wasn't reading, she spent those brief moments filling the pages of her blank notepad with her own poetry, wondering all the time if anything better lay ahead of her. Wasn't there more to life than tediously attending to the looms for ten hours each day?

For a moment, Adam had made her forget. Her breath had caught as she'd looked into his dark eyes, and when he smiled at her, he'd left her speechless. Lidia's foot plunged into a crusty pile of snow, bringing her back to reality. She shivered as the icy crystals tumbled into her boots. It was a chilling reminder of the truth of her situation.

Obviously Adam was no different from the scores of folks who disliked her simply because she was Polish, and now, without a family of her own, she had little interaction with others like her who had emigrated from her homeland. No matter what she did or how hard she worked to be a true lady of quality, things would never change. There was simply no place for her to find love in this New World.

THREE

The eighty-foot maple soared above him. Adam pressed the palms of his hands against the ridged bark of the tree and smiled, ready to continue the tradition of harvesting sap that had been done by men and women for centuries. A brisk westward wind blew, ruffling the hair on the back of his neck. Above him the sun shone bright, warming the day, but not enough to thaw the ground. The conditions were perfect.

For five winters he'd worked beside Old Man Potter, a no-nonsense codger who'd taught Adam everything he knew about the tedious process of gathering sap and the final process of turning the sap into syrup. After suffering from a bad case of pneumonia, Mr. Potter hadn't made it through the winter. To Adam's surprise he had left the entire farm to him.

This was the second year Adam worked the sugar brush alone. By next year, he hoped to be able to afford to hire a handful of men to gather an even larger amount of sap. And that wasn't all he planned. He was studying the profitability of using a portion of the land for horse breeding, or perhaps dairy farming. Something that would make the acreage self-sustaining.

Water dripped from an icicle at the top of the sugarhouse, then slid down the side of Adam's face. He shivered, not certain if it was from the cold or from the infection he'd been fighting for days. He simply didn't have time to be sick. He'd spent the past month repairing the furnace, vats, and other supplies at the sugar camp that was situated beside a small stream. Now that those preparations were finished, it was time to begin tapping the maple trees. Already he'd placed the taps into the trunks so he'd be ready for his first run tomorrow. The only thing left to do was to finish hanging the buckets that would in turn collect the maple sap.

He could almost taste the spread of sweet treats his stepmother would serve at the upcoming sugaring off, the annual celebration of the maple sugar harvest signaling the end of winter. Maple sugar on pancakes, maple cream, and caramelized sugar on snow would be plentiful as long as the weather cooperated. A bird chirped in the distance, and Adam sent up a short prayer that the Lord would hold off the warm weather this year. Spring might be coming, but not before his harvest had been collected.

He grabbed the last of the buckets from the back corner of the sugarhouse, pausing when he noticed a scrap of paper lodged in a crack in the wall. Curious, he knelt to pick it up. His heart sank when he realized what it was. Fingering the tattered photograph of Mattie was like a jolt from the past. He could still see the faraway look in his brother Samuel's eyes the day he'd sat on the stump down by the creek, the image of the girl he loved in his hands.

"I think I'm in love, Adam." Samuel had gazed at the photo like an infatuated schoolboy.

"You're too young to be in love." Adam's voice rang sharp with a note of truth, but he couldn't disguise his amusement. At sixteen, Samuel's head was in the clouds more often than not — and Mattie helped to keep it there.

"What about your dreams of becoming a doctor?" Adam leaned back against one of the maple trees, its flaming scarlet leaves reflecting its Creator's glory.

Samuel shrugged. "Mattie and I've talked about staying right here in Cranton and farming a bit of land once we're married —"

"So you've already talked about marriage?" Adam teased.

Samuel jumped from the stump, tackling Adam to the ground in one swift motion. Adam might have had the advantage of height as well as ten extra pounds, but Samuel was quicker. They rolled down the embankment, stopping only when they slammed into the side of a tree.

A wave of nausea swept over him, jerking Adam from the memories of carefree days that were no longer. With the image of his brother's lopsided grin still fresh in his mind, familiar feelings of anger seared through Adam's body as he stuffed the photo into his pocket.

Why did You let him die, God?

He pounded his fist against the wall of the sugarhouse. It was the question he longed to ask God face-to-face. If anyone should have died, it should have been him. As the eldest son in the family, he was responsible for his siblings. Failing to save his brother's life was worse than losing his own life.

Trying to ignore the growing dizziness, he yanked the last four buckets off the ground and headed for the maple grove where he would hang them. He had no choice but to make it though the next few weeks of the harvest. Maybe it was pride, like his father said, that had stopped him from accepting help from his family, but this was something he needed to do. A chance to prove to himself that he could succeed.

Five minutes later Adam hooked the last bucket onto one of the spouts he'd tapped into the tree. He took a staggering step, his vision blurring as he stumbled up the slight rise toward his cabin. He rubbed his eyes with the back of his hands then stared into the distance at the glistening snow. Maybe if he went to lie down for a few minutes he'd feel better. He shouldn't be surprised at how tired he felt. Besides preparing to harvest the sap, it had taken weeks of backbreaking work to make Old Man Potter's two-room cabin livable, and there were still a dozen things he planned to do once the harvest was over.

Like make it livable for a wife and a family.

The thought caught him off guard and brought with it vivid images of Lidia. Her long auburn hair and those sad eyes that made him long to find out what heart-wrenching secrets they held. Trying to erase the memory of holding her in his arms at

40

the base of the tree, he tugged at the collar of his shirt and made his way up the hill. The temperature had gradually warmed throughout the afternoon, but not enough to cause him to break out into a sweat. If he could just get to the cabin . . .

He stumbled toward the porch and tripped on a scrap piece of wood. Falling onto the ground, he felt the sharp impact of something hitting his head. He cried out in pain and watched the flow of crimson spill across the white snow.

Lidia shivered as she tramped through the snow, wondering what she could say to Koby that would knock some sense into him without deepening the silence that separated them. Her brother shuffled beside her, a sullen expression on his boyish face. At thirteen, he was as tall as she, and noticeably heavier. No longer a boy, yet still not a man.

She watched as he kicked the ground with the toe of his shoe. White powder flew in every direction. He might be mad at her for making him return to the mill, but she was furious that he'd run away. After a coworker informed her that Koby had left his work post in a huff, she'd spent two hours searching the surrounding woodlands. Just before the last curtain of night had fallen, she'd found him trudging down a narrow road.

Lidia worked to control her unsteady breathing. She was angry with him for jeopardizing their jobs. Angry with him for putting her in the position where she had to risk her life searching for him. The incident with the rabid dog had proven to be a reminder that it wasn't safe to wander these roads alone. It was time he thought about someone besides himself. Life might not be easy, but they were family. In order to survive, they were going to have to stick together.

"Why did you leave?" she asked, breaking the silence between them.

"What does it matter to you?"

She decided to ignore his defiant tone for now and worked instead to keep the frustration out of her own voice. "We're family. We have to be there for each other."

"I'm sorry."

"Sorry?" She stopped, choking back the stream of tears that threatened to flow. "Is that all you have to say? You scared me, Koby! If anything ever happened to you —"

"What do you want me to say?"

Lidia squeezed her eyes closed. *I don't know what to do anymore, God.*

Continuing her prayer for wisdom, she ran to catch up with him. His hands were stuffed in his pockets, and his head hung low. She'd heard him threaten numerous times to leave the strict confines of the mill, but she had always believed he realized the foolishness of such an act. Apparently, she'd been wrong. Still, part of her couldn't blame him. A boy his age ought to be out fishing with friends after school, but instead his lot was ten hours of manual labor every day.

Lidia paused at a fork in the road. Darkness hung over them, with only the glowing light of the full moon to lead their way. She didn't know the outlying areas, and it was obvious they were lost. At some point they had veered off the main road. The chilling howl of a dog broke through the night air, enveloping her in a cloak of fear. The snow had begun to fall, and she knew she'd never find her way back to the mill in these conditions. She had to find shelter.

Ten minutes later, with the snow flurries increasing, she caught sight of the silhouette of a cabin a couple hundred feet ahead of them. On a cold evening like tonight, smoke should be billowing from the chimney, but there wasn't even a hint of light shining though the windows. If no one was home, at least they could use it as a temporary shelter. It wasn't worth walking in circles all night trying to find their way back to the mill. They could freeze to death before morning.

She motioned to her brother, who solemnly followed her. As they came closer to the house, she noticed the dozens of buckets set up in the surrounding sugar brush, ready to collect the year's harvest of sap. For years, her father had spent the final weeks of winter working for various sugarhouses helping with the gathering of the sap. It was one of her favorite memories of her family. After the maple crop had been harvested, they gathered together for the sugaring off, where the children had been allowed to eat as much of the sweet syrup as they'd wanted.

Her foot struck something solid in the middle of the path, and she nearly stumbled.

Koby caught her, then knelt in the snow. "It's a man, Lidia."

She stopped, gazing down at the crumpled figure. More than likely the cad was drunk, but this man had made the unfortunate mistake of choosing the wrong place to consume his spirits.

Lidia bent to see if he was breathing then jerked back in surprise. Even in the darkening shadows of night, she recognized Adam. He was alive, and there was no smell of alcohol on his breath. After ripping off her gloves, she touched his forehead with the back of her hand. Fever raged through his body.

"Quick, Koby. Help me carry him into the house."

Grunting his disdain, her brother leaned over to grab Adam's shoulders. Lidia struggled under the weight of his limp body. Somehow they managed to move him past the slick steps and into the only bedroom of the cabin.

They laid him on the wool blanket that covered the bed, then, after lighting a lantern, she instructed her brother to get a fire going. The first thing she had to do was determine the severity of the head wound, then warm him up. Searching the confines of the small cabin for fresh water and a cloth, she was surprised at how orderly the room was. While simply furnished, each piece was solid and well built. All it needed were a few extra touches that only a woman could provide. Curtains to grace the windows, colorful rugs to adorn the floor, and perhaps a handmade quilt to cover the bed . . .

And you foolishly dare to imagine that you could ever be that woman?

Frowning at the unwanted thought, she took the wet cloth and sat beside Adam, carefully wiping the wet blood from his forehead. He groaned and opened his eyelids.

"Li . . . Lidia?" He smiled at her, but his voice was unsteady. "I was dreaming about you." Clearly he was delirious.

"Be still. You're burning with fever, and I need to clean your wound."

"No, I'm not, it's just . . ." He struggled to get up.

She eased him back down on the bed and finished washing away the blood. While he was going to have quite a lump, it didn't look too serious. More worrisome were his fever and the fact that he had likely spent several hours lying on the cold ground. If they hadn't come along when they had . . .

"You don't understand." This time Adam fought harder to sit up. "I have to check the buckets. It's time for the sap to run."

From the pale light of the lantern, she could see splotches of red across his face from the cold. He was in no condition to get out of bed, let alone work. She laid him back against the pillow. Thankfully, he was too weak to resist her any longer.

"Don't worry about your sap collection." She wrung the cloth into a bowl. "You're not getting out of this bed."

It was a choice between her employment

and the livelihood of this man, but as soon as she'd spoken, Lidia knew she'd already made her decision. With weather conditions the way they were, she didn't dare try to go for help. And that left her with one option.

She knew how grueling the process was. Harvesting the sap was only the beginning of the timely process. Once collected, the fresh sap had to be boiled immediately into syrup. Winter would not wait for Adam to recover. She and Koby would have to harvest the sap.

FOUR

Lidia ran her finger down the rough bark of the maple tree then across the tip of the spout where a clear liquid dripped into the bucket below. The bulge of an icicle remained on the tap, confirming that the conditions for the harvest of the sweet sap were perfect. At first, Adam had tried to fight her decision to begin the gathering in the maple grove, insisting he was well enough to do the work himself. She watched as he stumbled across the room in search of his boots, until he finally conceded that he wasn't well enough to get up, let alone work out in the chilly March afternoon. In his feverish state, he'd been forced to lie back down and, within minutes, had fallen into a restless sleep against his thick feather pillow.

Now the wind whipped through the grove, leaving a stinging sensation in Lidia's cheeks. The snow glistened beneath the pale sun, shimmering like tiny crystals through the maple grove. It wasn't cold enough to freeze the sap, but it was cold enough for the wind to make its way through the threads of her thin coat.

Balancing the half-full bucket between both hands, she tromped through the crusty snow toward the next tree. By nightfall, the buckets would be heavy with sap. How Adam had ever thought he could collect then boil the sap while keeping the fires going by himself, she had no idea.

In the short time she'd been around him, he'd reminded her of her father. Stubborn, yet enthusiastic at the same time. Her father had possessed a passion for freedom. This deep emotion had sustained him through difficult times in his native country, through the long crossing of the Atlantic with their family, and to the new life they started together in America. She wasn't sure what drove Adam. Part of her wanted to know what lay behind those dark eyes. Another part of her wanted to run.

Koby labored without complaint, a feat considering his normal attitude at the mill and the work that still lay ahead of them. Once they collected the sap and transferred it into the large vats at the sugarhouse, the liquid would have to be constantly stirred

49

as it boiled, making sure it didn't run over or form a skin on the surface. With the furnace burning strong, the entire process would have to be repeated tomorrow and the next day — as long as Adam needed them or until the weather cleared enough for one of them to go for help.

Lidia was used to hard work. She hung an empty bucket, swapping it for the fuller one. For a moment, Mrs. Moore's birdlike nose and thin, wrinkled face flashed before her. While the woman who ran the factory where they worked wasn't as stern as many of the overseers she'd heard about, Lidia knew she wouldn't tolerate their absence. But neither could Lidia ignore the fact that Adam needed her. A good run of sap wouldn't wait for the deep snow to melt from the roads or for Adam to regain his strength.

Her brother struggled beside her as he strained to lift the wooden sap yoke that carried the two buckets across his shoulders. "Do you remember the last sugaring off we went to?"

"I remember how you ate so many sour pickles we all thought you'd turn green." Lidia laid the bucket down then leaned against one of the sturdy trees, smiling at the memories.

The pickles were said to cut the sweetness

of the sugar so one could eat plenty. Koby had never had any problem eating a generous amount of the waxy, taffylike treat that had been boiled then cooled into strips on the snow and eaten with a fork.

She wrapped her arms around herself and let out a slow sigh. "We had some good times together as a family, didn't we?"

Her brother kicked one of the buckets with the tip of his foot. "I miss them."

"I miss them, too, Koby."

Her brother's pained expression sifted though the recesses of her heart. *What do I say to make things better for him, God?* She longed for her mourning to turn into joyful dancing, as David once wrote in the Old Testament. Longed to see a carefree smile cross her brother's lips. But it was something she hadn't seen for months. Or felt in her own life.

"Do you ever think what life might be like if they hadn't died?"

Lidia cleared her throat at her brother's question, unable to stop the sudden flood of emotions that overtook her and brought the sting of tears to her eyes. "You know thinking like that won't bring them back. All we can do is make the best of what we have."

Koby folded his arms across his chest, his

chin set in fierce determination. "You could always marry someone like the mister inside. He might not be rich, but he's got all this land. Maybe he wouldn't mind having a boy like me around if I was extra good. I'd work hard so he wouldn't have any reason to send me away. It would almost be like having a family again —"

"Koby!"

"What's wrong with my dreaming about having something gooder?"

"Something better." Lidia frowned. She couldn't blame him for wishing things were different. It was something she did, as well. But in reality, sometimes life handed you a plate of sour pickles instead of a huge iron vat of sweet maple syrup. No gallant hero was going to sprint from the pages of a legend and into her life to change her situation. She had to pull them through herself — that was what *Americans* did.

"What about you?" Koby took a step forward. "Don't you want more out of life than working ten hours a day for some overseer who doesn't care anything about us, except that we can get the work done so they can make more money?"

"Koby, you —"

"Well, it's true, ain't it?"

"Isn't it?" Lidia shut her mouth at the attempt to correct her brother's grammar. Perfect speech and fine manners would never really change who they were. She'd found that out firsthand. Their parents had worked for a dozen years to establish themselves as hardworking American citizens who could provide for their family in ways they never could have in the old country. And they had achieved much of what they'd dreamed.

She'd seen the look of pride in her father's eyes when he returned from work with a piece of penny candy for each of his children. Her mother would scold him for spoiling them, but her eyes couldn't hide her own feelings of thankfulness for the blessings God had showered upon them. Life had been good.

But all that had changed. It had only taken the dreaded cholera a matter of days to rob her parents of life and in turn change Koby and Lidia's future forever. With the loss of her father's income, she and her brother had become nothing more than immigrant factory workers. It was useless to spend her life dreaming about things changing. Someone like Adam would never choose a girl like her. Fairy tales like that didn't happen in real life.

"It's time to get back to work, Koby."

53

Swallowing the lump in the back of her throat, Lidia picked up her bucket, stiffened her shoulders, and resolved to forget the past and concentrate only on the matter at hand. Saving Adam Johnson's maple crop.

Adam rolled over onto his side then winced at the sharp pain that splintered behind his eyes. Reaching up to feel the throbbing knot on his head, he struggled against someone's hand pressing down on his shoulder.

"Please. Lie back, and I'll get you some broth to drink."

He opened his eyes and let them adjust to the fading shadows in the room. Something simmered on the stove, making his mouth water. How long had it been since he'd eaten? He focused on the figure leaning over him. The final rays of the evening sun filtered into the room, bathing Lidia's face in the soft light and causing him to wonder if he was simply dreaming about the fairy-like girl who fluttered in and out of his dreams.

Adam pushed his elbows against the bed and tried to sit up again. The pain that seared through him confirmed he was awake.

"Not so fast." Lidia felt his forehead with the back of her hand. "Your fever broke a couple hours ago, but that doesn't mean you can get up."

"I feel fine. Just a bit achy."

She rested her fists against her hips and frowned. "You might be feeling better, but after three days in bed with a raging fever and a bump the size of Massachusetts on your head, I think —"

"Wait a minute." Adam studied the swoosh of her skirts as she moved away from his bed. At times he'd been aware of her presence as she hovered around him with a cool cloth and cups of water for him to sip. But he thought he'd been dreaming. "What did you say?"

"You've been sick."

"I know, but how long?"

She paused beside the rickety table he needed to refurbish. There were so many things he'd intended to do.

"My brother and I found you lying outside on the ground three days ago. I'm not sure how long you were sick before that."

Adam's stomach clenched. A few more hours lying against the frozen ground and more than likely he wouldn't have made it. But three days passing meant that three days of harvesting his sap was lost.

Struggling to ignore the ache that engulfed every muscle of his body, he forced himself to sit up. Sick or not, he had work to do. "I've got to get up. My maple crop —"

"My brother and I have been harvesting the sap in the mornings and afternoons." Lidia stopped in the doorway of his room and turned to face him. "The run slowed down a bit last night as the temperatures dropped too low, but the sun was out today and the taps ran well again. You're going to have a great crop this year."

Adam's jaw tightened. It wasn't as if he didn't appreciate the effort, but there was so much more to gathering the sap than simply emptying the buckets. A novice trying to do the work would ruin the entire season's production. "You don't understand, the sap has to be boiled —"

"Of course." Lidia tilted her head. "Koby's kept the fire going strong. Thankfully you had plenty of wood for fuel."

"But do you know how to test the density of the sap when you're boiling it? Once the sap begins to drip off the end of the dipper in sheets —"

"Then it's syrup. It's called aproning." He watched through the doorway as she busied herself in the kitchen then returned with a cup of the broth he'd smelled simmering on the stove. "My father used to work in the maple groves at the end of every winter, and

I helped him."

The room seemed to spin around him. "I don't understand. Why are you doing this for me?"

"There wasn't much of a choice. Since I don't know this area well, I was afraid I wouldn't find my way back to town with the snowdrifts and the weather being the way it is. Once it clears, my brother and I can go and find a few men to help, but until then, we couldn't let your sap go bad, now could we?"

He fingered the edge of his worn blanket. "It's not that I don't appreciate what you've done, but I can't have you and your brother working my maple crop for me."

"And why not? You'll never get well if you don't get your strength back, and either we do the work or buckets sit full of wasted sap." Lidia's eyes brightened with her smile. "Drink some of this broth and stop worrying. Fretting over things you can't do anything about will only make you grow old quicker, as my babcia used to say."

"Your who?" Adam took a sip of the broth and felt the warmth of the liquid run down his throat.

"My grandmother. You'd have liked her. She was almost as stubborn as you are."

He shook his head at the comment then

winced as the pain returned. Whether he wanted to admit it or not, it did seem as if his stubbornness had once again gotten him into trouble. If he'd listened to his father, he would have the help he needed instead of having to rely on a young girl who barely weighed more than a feather. The days might be warming up, but she had no business working out there. Harvesting a maple crop was hard work.

Ignoring the guilt that surged through him, he tried to stand, determined to get out of bed. He crossed the wood-planked floor in uneven steps.

Lidia grabbed his arm. "You're too weak to get out of bed."

"I'm fine." His jaw tensed. "Just let me sit in the other room for a while, then I promise to go back to bed."

"Suit yourself."

He watched as Lidia bustled around his kitchen. He had plans to sand the cupboards and replace the stove, but time hadn't allowed it. There had been so much work to do, and the kitchen had never been a priority. Suddenly, he wished he'd made it a priority.

Lidia pulled a pan out of the oven, and the yeasty aroma of freshly baked bread wafted to him. It and the fragrant broth were much more alluring than the smells of burnt biscuits and stale coffee that normally filled the room. He had no problem fixing beans and overdone biscuits in his kitchen, but he'd certainly never stopped to consider what a woman might think about his living conditions.

"I'm sorry about the kitchen." He cleared his throat. "It wasn't exactly built with the needs of a woman in mind. The supplies are a bit low. . . ."

"I've managed to make do." She waved her hand in his direction. "Once you're up and around, you'll need something hearty to eat like a steaming pot of *bigos,* though you're right. Your store of food is completely inadequate, even if it is just for one man."

"Bigos?"

"Stew. My father could never understand how a man could survive without a steamy bowl of stew on the table at night. It's full of different meats and vegetables." She dried her hands on a dishcloth. "I'll make you a huge pot one day, and you can taste it for yourself."

She must have realized how intimate her comment might be interpreted because Adam caught her sheepish expression after she'd said it. Her cheeks reddened as she turned away from him, pushing a strand of auburn hair out of her face. Once he got out of bed, she would leave and there would be no reason for her to ever make him another meal. His pulse quickened despite his earlier resolve to forget her.

"Tell me about your family," he said.

Lidia shrugged as she finished washing the dishes. "There's not much to tell. My parents emigrated from Poland to America when I was six. I never saw my grandmother again."

He could hear the marked sadness in her voice. "And your parents?"

"They died during a cholera outbreak a little over a year ago. Now it's just me and my brother."

"I'm sorry."

"There's no sense in dwelling on the past." She shook her head, as if trying to erase the memories inside. "What about your family?"

"My parents live a few miles from here on a farm where I was raised with my brothers and sisters." He cleared his throat. "There's seven of us now. Samuel was killed last fall."

"I'm sorry. You must miss him tremendously."

"I do."

As much as he appreciated Lidia's and her brother's help, he couldn't help thinking of his own brother. The deafening sound of a gun firing. His brother lying dead on the street. Anger welled within him at the memories. He knew his sister Rebecca was right. It wasn't fair to blame an entire people for one man's wrong, and he knew Lidia had nothing to do with his brother's death. But knowing the truth and stopping the anger inside him had proved to be two different things.

Part of him wanted to reach out and comfort her for her own losses. To tell her that everything was going to be all right despite the horrible heartache she'd lived through. The other part of his soul still grappled over what he'd lost. There was no way around it. Seeing Lidia only reminded him of his own pain and his own guilt in allowing it to happen.

Struggling to remain sitting up, he fought against the growing nausea. While he appreciated Lidia and Koby's help, he needed to find a way to finish the job — alone.

FIVE

Adam shoved his boots on before stepping out onto the porch. The morning sun greeted him, a pale circle against a white sky. He pulled up the collar of his jacket against the wind, not needing to look at a thermometer to know the temperature wasn't rising fast enough. And if he was reading the sky correctly, a storm was coming in. Though it wasn't unusual for cold snaps or warm days to temporarily stop the run of sap, he was anxious that the weather conditions hold for at least another two weeks so he could collect his entire run this year. He already had a buyer lined up for his syrup, and he would need every bit of cash he could earn in order to continue with his expansion plans for the land.

He rubbed his hand against the side of his head, thankful that the swelling had gone down. After another two days of recovering, he'd made no promises to Lidia that he would stay in bed as she and her brother had slipped outside to begin another day of harvesting. Even if the sap weren't running, there would still be plenty of work to do. Supplies needed to be scalded to prevent the syrup from spoiling; necessary repairs to the buckets and other equipment would need to be made, as well as extra wood chopped for the fire.

Lidia rounded the corner of the house with two buckets in her hands, stopping when she saw him. "Adam. I thought you were sleeping."

"I couldn't stay in bed another minute." He read the look of concern in her eyes as her brow furrowed, and he forced a grin. "I'm fine. Really. And I'm ready to get back to work. A man can only stay cooped up in that cabin for so long."

"You're still weak." She set the buckets on the porch and started up the steps. "And you need to eat something."

"I already did. I found the leftover biscuits you made. Tasted as good as my step-mother's, which is saying something. She's a fantastic cook."

"I'm glad you liked them." He caught her familiar blush as she spoke and couldn't help but warm at her smile. "I'm sure you felt the cold snap last night, and the temperature's not warming up like it needs to. I'm not sure how much we'll be able to collect."

He'd expected her to tell him that he needed to march back inside the house and get back in bed, but apparently she'd decided not to argue with him today. He was glad, even though she'd probably be right.

He leaned his palms against the porch rail. "A break in the weather will give me a chance to get caught up."

Lidia picked up the empty buckets and started across the snow toward the grove of stately maple trees. He followed her through the sugar brush, amazed at her endurance. He had poured so much of who he was into this land and knew the backbreaking effort it took to harvest the sap.

The buckets hung from each tree waiting to collect the sweet liquid. Some of the trees spanned almost four feet in diameter. Others were much smaller, but Old Man Potter had told him they were all at least forty years old.

"Did you know that as the tree grows, the bark doesn't expand with it? You can see how it keeps splitting open." Adam ran his hand across the shaggy bark. "These trees are as individual as people."

She came to stand beside him. "Meaning?"

"One might produce sap that is consistently sweeter than the others while another's sap might taste like water. And their sap runs differently, as well. Some manage a good run every year and others might produce a lot less."

"Who taught you about the harvest?"

"Old Man Potter owned this property. I started working for him when I was about fourteen, and while he was a bit of a codger, he became like a grandfather to me." Adam smiled at the memory of the gray-haired man who had been an active part of every harvest until the year he died. "He taught me the science of tapping a tree for the best results, how to study the bark as well as the new growth, and where to set the buckets. When he died, he left me the land."

"That's quite an inheritance."

"I suppose I was the grandson he never had. While he never told me, rumor has it his only son was killed in a gunfight back in Kansas in the '50s."

"You must have meant a lot to him, then."

"He meant a lot to me, too." He fidgeted, uncomfortable with the way the conversation had turned. "You know, if I close my eyes I can almost taste the syrup."

Lidia's eyes lit up when she smiled. "This has always been my favorite time of the year."

"Mine, too." As he lifted one of the buckets off the tree, he was surprised at how much he enjoyed her company. "It's crazy, I guess, but while my brother dreamed of being a doctor, my dreams always centered around God's good earth and the things I could produce with it."

"That's not a crazy dream. I think that's why I love poetry. Much of it describes nature so beautifully."

"Do you write your own?"

"Poetry?" Lidia lowered her gaze at the question. "When I find the time. I have a book where I write down thoughts and ideas, though my attempts certainly couldn't compare to some of the great poets of our time."

"Who said they had to?"

Adam tried to ignore the stirring of his heart when he looked at her, but he couldn't. What was it about Lidia that set his senses alive when he was around her? From the first time he'd looked into her dark mahogany eyes and caught the rosy blush that swept across her fair cheeks, she'd affected him like no woman ever had.

The wall he'd put up around him was

beginning to crack. He was now able to see Lidia as an individual person, not simply a Polish immigrant.

"What's your favorite kind of maple syrup?" Lidia's abrupt change in subject amused him. While she emitted a certain confidence, at the same time he sensed a streak of vulnerability within her. And that only made her more captivating.

Adam smiled at the question. "Without a doubt, maple cream. Spread it on a piece of hot bread and it's like a bit of heaven right there in your hand."

"That's my favorite, too. That and a tall stack of pancakes dripping with hot syrup. Then there's the music and singing at the annual sugaring off."

"While I've never been much on social gatherings, you do have a point."

Lidia laughed, then picked up one of the buckets filled with sap. "Do you feel like walking to the sugarhouse? Or would you rather take the wagon?"

"It's not far. I'll walk."

Five minutes later, Adam stepped out of the chilly breeze that blew through the maple grove and into the warmth of the sugarhouse. The aroma of hot syrup lingered in the air from the sap that was being boiled down. Taking in a deep breath, he felt his body relax. There was something about this first rite of spring that always invigorated him. Looking at the bubbling vats, he saw that everything had been done exactly as needed.

"I don't know what to say. I'm amazed at how much you've accomplished."

Koby stood in the corner of the room stirring the sap.

Adam reached out his hand toward the boy. "I don't think I've thanked you properly for what you've done, young man."

Koby shook his hand and cracked a smile. "It's better than working for the old crow at the factory —"

"Koby!" Lidia's eyes widened.

"Well, it's true." The boy went back to stirring the hot liquid in slow, circular strokes. "She's not exactly the friendliest overseer in the world."

"She's always been good to us, Koby, and you know it."

Adam paused, confused. "You work in one of the factories?"

Lidia played with the folds of her skirt and nodded.

Why should he be surprised? A majority of immigrants worked in the factories. Adam swallowed hard, realizing for the first time that their sacrifice to help him ran far deeper than just the physical strain involved. "They'll fire you for this."

"Probably." She bit her lip.

Koby took a step toward him. "Trust me, it's no great loss, Mr. Johnson. There are other factories looking for workers, unless you'd like to hire us for the rest of the season. There's plenty of work that could be done here —"

"Koby, that's not appropriate for you to ask." Lidia kept her words low and steady, but there was an obvious hint of pride behind her statement.

"Fine." The boy's dark brow puckered. "Like I said, there are other factories in the area willing to take advantage of us like the old . . . I mean Mrs. Moore."

"I wish I could offer to hire you both." Adam cleared his throat, not knowing how to respond to the boy. "I'm just not sure how I could pay —"

"Of course not." Lidia whispered something to her brother before moving to empty one of the buckets into the vat. "We would never want to put you in such an awkward position. We'll be fine. Right now, all we need to worry about is the work before us."

Adam cringed. He'd never given a second thought to the conditions of the surrounding factories that dotted the state. Even with new laws that limited the number of hours children were allowed to work, he knew that the labor was hard, rules stringent, and the pay minimal. It wasn't the kind of place he wanted to see Lidia working in — or Koby. But he knew that even if he wanted to hire them for the rest of the season, he simply didn't have the means to pay them. If they lost their jobs on top of everything else . . .

"Let me speak to Mrs. Moore on your behalf." Adam caught her troubled gaze. "Once I explain what happened, I'm sure she'll be sympathetic."

Lidia shrugged a shoulder. "It might make a difference, but please don't worry about us. We'll be fine."

She smiled at him, and his heart pounded. She looked small and vulnerable beside the large iron vat. He shouldn't feel this way. Something inside him made him want to protect her. To gather her into his arms and promise her everything would be all right.

A wave of nausea swept over him, and he leaned against the wall for support.

Lidia grabbed his arm and led him to a wooden bench in the corner of the room. "You're not strong enough yet."

"I'm fine. It's just a dizzy spell."

"No, it's not. You've overdone it." Lidia glanced up at her brother. "If the snow melts enough by morning, we'll go into town for help."

"Didn't you know? All Polish fairy tales have at least one dragon." Lidia laughed as she leaned closer to the fire that crackled in the stone fireplace of Adam's small cabin.

He sat across from her, his eyes twinkling with mischief. "And like the story you just told, are the princesses always rescued by handsome heroes?"

"Of course, just like the stories you tell in this country."

Two more days had passed, and Lidia found herself wanting to suspend their time together indefinitely. Tonight the stars loomed bright overhead, signaling an end to the gray, overcast skies and below-normal temperature that had stopped the flow of sap.

While they had waited for the daytime temperatures to rise, Lidia spent the long days scalding the utensils for the sap harvest, while her brother ensured there was plenty of wood to keep the vats of sap boiling. Adam had worked intermittently as he slowly regained his strength, repairing the handles of several of the buckets when he wasn't resting or engaging in snowball fights with her brother.

Adam's cheeks had lost their pasty appearance, and it was becoming clear he wouldn't need her much longer. Besides that, now that he was up and around again, it wouldn't be proper for her to stay even with her brother beside her.

It was time to go into town to find someone to help Adam with the rest of the harvest. Then she would return to the factory where she could only pray Mrs. Moore would graciously agree to keep her and her brother on as employees.

Koby snored softly beside her on the small couch. She put her arm around him and pulled him close. In spite of the hard work he'd accomplished, she hadn't missed seeing how he'd thrived this past week. Being outside in the fresh air, away from the demanding labor of the factory, had done wonders for him. She'd seen him smile for the first time in months, something even she hadn't been able to get him to do before.

Adam had a way with him, as well. Lidia was convinced he'd gotten out of bed sooner than he should have, but even in his weakened state, he seemed to find the energy to encourage her brother. And now she would have to take Koby away from all of this.

Something cried out from the darkness

beyond the cabin.

"What was that?"

Adam cocked his head. "Sounded like an owl."

"No." She leaned forward and put a finger to her lips.

She listened carefully as an animal rummaged in the trees. "Are there animals that might get into the buckets?"

"Might be. I'll go check it out."

"I'm coming with you."

The front door creaked open, and she followed Adam across the porch and down the steps, careful not to slip on the remnants of ice that encrusted the wooden boards as she worked to stay in the light of the lantern he held above his head.

"Could be a wildcat," he whispered. "But I doubt it."

Lidia shivered and wondered if she should run back to the safety of the cabin.

Adam shone the light up into one of the trees and caught the reflection of two round eyes. "I was right. It's an owl."

"Are you sure?" She still wasn't convinced. "What I heard sounded much bigger."

Adam laughed. "There's nothing to worry about. We get a few wild animals around here, but none of them have ever made a menace of themselves so far."

"I hope not."

"Look at the stars." Adam blew out the lantern and gazed toward the heavens. The night sky was so bright the extra light wasn't needed. "My father and I used to lie out in the fields in the summertime where he'd teach me the names of many of the great constellations."

"It is beautiful." She looked up at him and tried to ignore the flutter of her heart over his nearness. "Maybe we should go in now. You must be exhausted after today."

Adam drew in a deep breath. "I do need to shake this lingering fatigue. If the temperatures rise like I think they will after I get you off to town, I'm going to have a busy day tomorrow."

The reminder that she wouldn't be a part of his days anymore saddened her. "We could stay longer, my brother and I . . ."

"I wouldn't ask that of you. I'm already worried about your job at the factory."

He was right. She knew they had to leave, but the thought left her sober. Tomorrow she would be gone. She wasn't sure when she'd ever see him again.

Lidia turned and twisted her ankle on a broken limb. Struggling to keep her balance, she felt his strong hand envelop her arm and hold her upright. "Thank you. I'm fine."

She caught his gaze and for a moment time hovered motionless around her. She had no right feeling what she did toward him. They lived in two different worlds. She was a second-generation immigrant. A factory worker. He came from a successful family and owned his own land —

"Lidia . . ."

Before she could say anything, his lips pressed against hers. She felt breathless and lightheaded. Hadn't she daydreamed of him holding her and telling her he cared for her? And now his arms surrounded her.

He stepped back abruptly. "I'm sorry. I don't know what I was thinking. I had no right to kiss you."

She smiled up at him. "It's all right. Really."

Heat rose in her cheeks, and she was certain he could read her thoughts. While he'd been in his feverish state, she'd dared imagine what it would be like to care for him as his wife. Dared to imagine that something could ever come about between them, and now wasn't that very possibility looming before her? Surely this wasn't really happening.

"It's late." He ran his thumb down her jawline. "We'll talk more in the morning."

Following closely behind him, she stepped

into the cabin and watched as Adam entered his room and shut the door behind him. With a smile on her face, she sat down beside her sleeping brother, wondering all the time what tomorrow might bring.

Lidia arose early the next morning, careful not to disturb her brother as she went about the morning chores in the small cabin one last time. She smiled as she chopped up the potatoes and fried them, remembering her dreams filled with Adam and the softness of his touch. She longed to know more about the man she'd diligently nursed back to health over the past few days. It seemed unbelievable that he might care for her.

Standing in front of the kitchen window that overlooked the maple grove, she flipped the last of the pancakes in the hot pan as the morning sun began to peek above the horizon. Not only had she decided to prepare a decent breakfast for Adam, she also wanted to make sure everything was in order before he took them to the mill this morning. It was the least she could do.

Or maybe it was simply because she wanted to prolong her time here. But the dark clouds that had hovered above them the past few days had vanished, and with Adam's health returning, there was no excuse for her to stay.

With the pancakes cooked and the potatoes nearly finished, she quickly worked to tidy up the room. Dusting the wooden bookshelf, a small stack of newspaper clippings fluttered to the floor. She picked them up, then froze as she glanced at the familiar face.

"Jarek."

She hadn't spoken the name of her older brother for almost a year and a half. Her family hadn't known anything until her father had happened to see the sketch of his eldest son in the post office — wanted for murder. Jarek had been missing for weeks and with a bounty on his head; none of her family believed they'd ever see him again.

She scanned the paper, which told briefly about the incident. Here, in black and white, were the details she'd tried to forget during the months that followed her father's discovery. Then her parents died, bringing another fresh wave of grief. A name caught her attention. One of the details she'd apparently chosen to forget. But this time the named burned across her heart. Her brother, Jarek, had murdered Samuel Johnson.

Six

Lidia crinkled the paper between her fingers and let the sketch of her brother drop to the floor. It was happening again. Feelings of panic, grief, and helplessness washed over her in a single wave. She remembered the day they learned the truth about why Jarek had run away. Father had sat her and Mother down and told them what he'd seen in town, revealing the awful truth that a thousand dollars was being offered for the capture of her brother.

Her mother had refused to believe the accusations that Jarek had killed someone. Lidia hadn't wanted to believe them either, yet she'd seen the way his temper flared, time and time again, with little provocation. Then there was the fact that her father's gun was missing. Her father hadn't told her mother, but Lidia had opened the empty case and at that moment realized the accusations were true. Her brother was a murderer.

Until today, she'd never really stopped to think about the family of the young man Jarek killed. At the beginning she'd felt sorry for them, wishing she could go back in time and change things, but all she'd known was that someone had died. He'd been a nameless person she couldn't put a face to, and her own grief in losing her brother was still too new. Now the family had a name. Her heart ached for Adam.

Lidia straightened the papers and shoved them back inside the cabinet. She'd seen the pain in Adam's eyes when he spoke about his brother. Even after almost a year and a half, the pain ran deep. She could sense the closeness the two men had shared. It hurt her to know how much he'd lost. She could imagine that feeling all too well. Because on the day Jarek took Samuel's life, she lost her own brother, as well.

The smell of something burning filled her nostrils. She hurried across the room, barely scooping the pan off the stove in time to save the potatoes from scorching. She shoved the buckwheat pancakes and salvaged fried potatoes onto a pan and into the oven to warm, letting the door bang shut.

The crude drawing of her brother's face was etched in the back of her mind. That wasn't how she wanted to remember him. She wanted to destroy the newspaper article and the heated accusations and put it all behind her as if it had never happened. Nothing, though, could change the reality of what had taken place between Jarek and Adam's brother.

There had been a time when things had been different with Jarek. Before he'd started running around with the wrong crowd. Before Lidia began to notice his anger simmering under the surface. Maybe if her parents had been stricter with him, he would have realized what he was doing, or if she had found the right words to say to him . . . But she knew that wasn't true. Jarek had been eighteen. The choices her brother made were his choices, not hers or her parents'.

She began washing the table in vigorous circles, remembering how her father decided not to tell the sheriff that he knew the once-innocent lad portrayed on the wanted poster. "What does it really matter?" he'd asked her mother as he wiped away her tears. They didn't have any information as to where he was. Even if they did, how could a father turn his eldest son over to a hangman's noose?

As much as it hurt, she'd known deep

inside that she'd never see Jarek again. He was on the run from the law. Coming home wasn't an option. She didn't even know if he was alive. Had he somehow heard about the sudden death of their parents, or even begun to understand the tragedy he'd caused the Johnson family in losing their son?

Why did it have to be Adam's brother, Lord?

The truth was impossible for her to deal with. Glancing across the small living quarters, she felt as if the room were mocking her. There was no chance for her and Adam. She'd lost him before ever really getting to know him. She'd seen the way he looked into her eyes in the moonlight. The wide grin that crossed his face as he dared to steal a kiss. In her amazement over it all, she knew without a doubt that she felt the same way. She'd dared to wonder if there was a chance for him to fall in love with her.

But now it didn't matter what Adam felt toward her. All that was about to change. He would never look at her that way again once he found out the truth about her brother.

Running the back of her hand across her lips, she could still feel the sweetness of his kiss. It had been wrong to think there could ever be anything between them.

Wondering where Lidia and her brother were, Adam stepped out of his room and into the kitchen. The appetizing smells of buckwheat pancakes and fried potatoes filled his senses as he peeked into the oven at the breakfast Lidia had prepared. How she'd managed to transform his meager supplies into such a mouthwatering meal, he had no idea. He'd never had the opportunity to eat with her during his recovery and didn't intend to lose this chance to be with her one last time before she left.

Sighing, he shut the oven door. All he could think about was the unsettling truth that he had to take them back to the mill this morning. He cringed at the thought of Lidia working day after day for some calloused overseer who didn't care when she got tired or hungry or if she simply wanted to spend an afternoon reading poetry. She didn't deserve to live such a harsh life. She needed a home and a family where she could feel safe and secure. But it was more than just the conditions of the factory that bothered him. After their kiss, he realized how much he didn't want to see her go. And how much he was going to miss her.

He'd never intended to kiss her, but even

in that brief moment he'd delighted in her touch and her closeness. Yet he'd realized something else, as well. Lidia was an honorable woman with high moral standards. A stolen kiss in the moonlight wasn't the way to win a lady's heart. He wanted to proclaim his feelings to her, then ask permission to court her properly.

Adam stepped out onto the porch where he finally caught a glimpse of Lidia carrying buckets across the edge of the maple grove. He'd never expected her to work this morning. For the first time since the day she found him in the snow, he felt strong and ready to finish the job at hand. He wanted to take care of her. Not have to depend on her hard work for the survival of the farm.

He took the porch steps two at a time, realizing that Rebecca had been right. His anger toward one man shouldn't have anything to do with his feelings for Lidia. He sensed that she was uncomfortable with her position in life, but the fact that she worked in a mill didn't matter to him. There were so many things about her that amazed him. He'd watched her take a chance at losing her own means of livelihood for a stranger, seen her care for her brother, and witnessed her faith in God. This was the kind of woman he wanted to spend the rest of his life with.

He had no way of knowing if Lidia would be the woman he brought home as his wife one day, but he at least wanted the opportunity to find out. Before he took her in to town, he would make an opportunity to talk to her and see if there was a chance she felt the same way toward him.

Feeling a resurgence of energy with each stride, Adam crossed the open yard that separated the cabin from the maple grove. "Lidia, there's no reason for you to work this morning. Have you eaten?"

She nodded her head, her gaze trained on her work. "I left plenty for you in the oven."

"I saw what you made. Thank you. It looked wonderful. I thought we could eat breakfast together. The three of us, of course."

Lidia nodded, but again she didn't look at him. "I'm sorry, but I'm not hungry. Koby's already down at the sugarhouse. We wanted to do what we could before you took us back to the mill. There's so much to —"

"Wait a minute." They'd laughed under the stars last night. He'd felt the warmth in her voice as they'd talked to each other, but now her greeting seemed colder than the frozen ground beneath them. "What's wrong, Lidia?"

Her eyes widened. "Why do you ask?"

"I don't know. I just thought . . ." Adam paused. Perhaps he'd read her wrong last night and her response to his kiss had been nothing more than a figment of his imagination. Or worse, he'd offended her by presuming she was interested in him.

He lowered his voice. "It's about the kiss, isn't it? I'm sorry. I never should have assumed that you —"

"That I'm interested in you?"

"Are you?" He closed his mouth.

"That doesn't matter anymore."

"You're not making any sense, Lidia. I know now that I was presumptuous in kissing you without stating clearly my intentions toward you, and I do apologize."

She shook her head and squeezed her eyes shut. "You're only going to make things harder —"

"I was wrong." He took a step forward, longing to take her into his arms and make things right again. "That's what I wanted to talk to you about. I don't want today to be the last time I see you. I want to call on you and get to know you better."

"That will never happen, Adam."

"Why not? I don't understand."

"It's your brother Samuel." Lidia leaned

against one of the trees. "I know who killed him."

"What?" The sugar brush began to spin around him. How could she know who Samuel's murderer was?

This time she looked him straight in the eye. "I never told you that I have another brother. His name is Jarek."

"What does he have to do with Samuel?"

She took a deep breath then blew it out slowly as if trying to steady her nerves. "Shortly after we moved here, he disappeared. All we could do was pray that God would protect him and bring him back to us. Then one afternoon my father saw a sketch of my brother on a wanted poster, and we found out that he was wanted for murder. I never heard the name of the boy he was accused of killing until I saw one of your newspaper clippings this morning while I was cleaning." Lidia clenched the material of her dress with her fists. "He's wanted for the murder of Samuel Johnson."

Adam felt as if he'd been punched in the gut. Surely he'd misunderstood what she said. It didn't make sense. Maybe he was sicker than he thought. Fever often signaled delirium. He ran his hand across his brow and felt the heavy beads of sweat. That's what it was. He was simply having a bad dream. Maybe if he closed his eyes and relaxed, he would dream about their kiss instead. That had been real. She'd been so close, so real. It had happened. He knew it, but this . . .

"Adam, did you hear what I said?"

"There must be some mistake." Adam shook his head and took a step back, not wanting to believe her.

"There's no mistake. My brother killed your brother."

He looked up at her. Her eyes were rimmed with tears and her cheeks were blotchy as if she'd been crying. He'd never meant to make her cry.

"His name is Jarek."

"Jarek." The earth spun faster. That had been his name, but . . . "No, Lidia, you're mistaken. It couldn't have been your brother."

"I've seen the sketches. There's no doubt. They look just like him." She picked up her bucket and headed for the wagon. Her tears had been replaced by a vacant expression. "We never saw him again after that day. At first, my mother believed he'd simply gone back to Boston where we'd lived. She'd hoped he'd return for Christmas, but when my father saw the drawing and the reward of a thousand dollars on his head, we knew we were wrong. He wasn't ever coming home again. At least not alive."

Adam stopped beside her at the wagon. "Lidia, I'm so sorry . . ."

He choked on the words. Anger seeped through his pores. For a moment he was there again. In the past. He squeezed his eyes shut, praying that the haunting memories would leave him, but they wouldn't. Instead they replayed over and over.

Samuel throwing the first punch. The other boy returning the blow. Adam had tried to stop them, but Samuel wouldn't listen as he ran out the back to the side street and across the deserted field. There hadn't been time to pull them apart. There was nothing he could do but watch as the boy drew a pistol from his holster, aimed it at his brother, and killed him.

Adam tried to steady his breathing as he looked at her, but his heart raced out of control. It shouldn't matter. The fact that Lidia's brother had been the one to kill Samuel had nothing to do with her or who she was. She hadn't pulled the trigger. She was only guilty of being his sister, a fact she certainly couldn't control.

He looked into her eyes and saw tears brimming in the corners. Her gaze begged him to understand. Begged him to forgive her for what had happened in the past between their brothers. He could forgive her, because in truth there was nothing to forgive. But the fact that her brother had been the one to take Samuel's life would always stand between them. How could it not?

SEVEN

Lidia stood and watched Adam stride toward the cabin, all the while willing her tears to disappear. The door slammed shut behind him and caused a thin layer of snow to slide off the roof and cascade onto the porch.

She'd known the moment she read Samuel Johnson's name in the paper that no matter what Adam's feelings toward her might be, nothing would ever be the same between them. And how could she blame him? Every time he looked at her, he would be reminded of what he'd lost.

She'd seen the pain reflected in Adam's eyes as he'd fought to take in the truth of what she told him. The flash of anger that crossed his face might not have been directed toward her, but she'd felt it all the same.

Why, Lord? Why do You allow things like this to happen?

She grabbed one of the buckets by its handle, not caring that the sugary liquid sloshed over the sides. Her breath rose in frothy waves in front of her, the coldness of the morning penetrating her lungs. All around her lay the fading beauty of winter. Trees reached toward the heavens, their limbs proclaiming praises to their Creator. Birds chirped in chorus around her, singing their sweet songs that would soon usher in the coming spring. It was a scene she never tired of. God's white blanket had covered His earth, keeping it dormant, but soon He would bring it to life again in a blaze of color with the vast arrangement of spring's flowers, green grass, and azure skies.

But today, in spite of the beauty around her, she couldn't sense God's presence.

"Lidia?"

Turning, she saw her brother coming toward her, his feet crunching though the last of winter's snow. "Is Mr. Johnson all right? I thought he'd be up by now."

She didn't want to feel anything, but her heart skipped a beat at the sound of his name. "He's in the house. I'm sure he'll be out to work soon. Remember he's still recovering from his illness."

She wouldn't mention the real reason he was in the cabin. Whether or not it had been the right thing, their parents had tried to shelter Koby from Jarek's actions. Koby knew his brother had run away, but he had no idea about the details surrounding his disappearance. He had enough to deal with in life without knowing his brother was wanted for murder.

"I need to get him back for yesterday." Koby leaned against the side of the wagon, a mischievous grin on his face. "The weather's warming. I thought we could have one more snowball fight before we leave and it all melts away."

"Not today." She shook her head. "I was just coming to get you. We need to be leaving now."

"Come on." Her brother's lips curled into a pout. "We have time. It's not like Mrs. Moore will let us come back anyway. Why can't we just stay until the harvest is over and then figure out what we're going to do?"

"I said it's time to go." She winced at the sharpness in her voice. "I'm sorry, but it wouldn't look right. Now that Adam is out of bed, we're not needed here anymore."

"He does need us." Koby folded his arms across his chest. "You're worried about going back to the mill, aren't you?"

She jutted her chin upward at the question. "I'm responsible for you, and with the

92

strong possibility that helping with the harvest has cost us our jobs —"

"He likes you."

"What?"

"Adam."

Lidia picked up two buckets that were full of sap and headed toward the wagon. "I really don't want to talk about him."

"Why not? Did you have a fight?"

"Yes — no." She closed her eyes, wishing her brother wasn't quite so curious . . . and right.

"So which is it?"

She spun around to face him. "It's complicated, Koby."

"What's so complicated about two people liking each other? You could marry him, and we could stay here and forget the past and that awful Mrs. Moore."

Lidia frowned. He was right about one thing. It was time for her to forget the past. And that meant leaving her feelings for Adam behind, as well. While she didn't regret helping him, the reality was she had probably lost her job. Still, staying here was not an option. There was always the possibility of answering an ad from the local paper for a mail-order bride. Those ads filled the pages these days, but the very thought of marrying for anything but love made her blood run cold. A better option would be if someone in town agreed to hire her, but that still left them needing a place to stay.

Adam wasn't the answer to her prayers as she'd briefly dared to hope, but perhaps their situation would turn out better for them after all. If she could get a position in town it would give her brother an opportunity to go to school, something she desperately wanted for him.

Koby stepped beside her and draped his arm around her shoulder. "Leaving the mill would mean no more of the cook's dinners. I love your cooking, and it's obvious that Mr. Johnson agrees —"

"Koby." Despite his persistence, she had to laugh. Leave it to her brother to say the right thing to make her smile. The food at the mills did leave much to be desired. She and her brother had come up with their own names for the bland, often unidentifiable dishes — mysterious macaroni pie, seafood surprise, peculiar pastries . . .

"Do we really have to go?"

Lidia glanced up at the cabin and swallowed the feelings of regret that threatened to surface. "Yes, Koby, it's time to go."

Adam stared at the thin pile of newspaper

articles he'd kept after his brother's death. He shouldn't have walked away from Lidia, but he'd been so afraid of losing control of his emotions. His reaction was far from godly, but at the moment he didn't care. He knew he should bury the incident and leave it in the past. He should even be relieved to find out who was responsible for Samuel's death. But nothing would bring Samuel back, and nothing would erase the pain or the guilt he felt over what happened.

Trying to hold back thoughts of revenge, he pulled his leather-bound Bible out of a drawer. The pages fell open to the Sermon on the Mount in the book of Matthew. He'd underlined the verses on forgiveness in chapter six, but as many times as he'd read them, forgiveness still seemed impossible to find.

Forgiveness toward Samuel's murderer? Or forgiveness toward myself?

Adam slammed the book shut at the question. He hated the feelings of guilt that plagued him. Wasn't it easier to lay the blame at the feet of the boy who killed Samuel?

And his entire family, as well?

Again the unwanted stab of conscience haunted him. At Lidia's confession he'd run like a frightened animal. It had been her brother who'd killed Samuel. He couldn't deny that truth.

The uninvited image of Lidia filled the recesses of his mind. Her wide, brown eyes and soft smile had touched something inside of him that had never been awakened before. He could hear the entertaining lilt of her voice and the tinkling sound of her laughter. But most of all he could feel the feather touch of her lips against his. He'd wanted that moment to last forever and had even wondered if she might be the one person he needed to make his life complete.

A fire blazed in the hearth, taking off the chill of the morning. He threw the papers into the fire and watched the orange flames lick hungrily at the added fuel. As the articles disintegrated before him, crackling into black ashes, he wondered if it were possible for his emotions to do the same. To not only forgive and forget, but to put the past and its horrible mistakes behind him. Wasn't Lidia worth taking a chance on? Wasn't she worth taking the time to get to know better despite what her brother had done to his family?

I just don't think I can do it, Lord.

The squeak of a wagon wheel broke into his thoughts and drew his attention to the window. His father stepped out of the flatbed wagon in front of the cabin.

Adam took a deep breath, wondering what he should tell his father. Knowing the identity of Samuel's murderer should make it easier for the sheriff and his men to find him. But in the process it would break Lidia's heart. That was something he didn't want to happen no matter what his conflicting feelings toward her were at the moment.

Adam opened the door, then paused in the entrance as his father took the porch steps two at a time to greet him. He'd been told a dozen times how closely he resembled his father with his coal-black hair and dark eyes with their hints of gold. He'd always longed to emulate his godly character, as well, something that at the moment was proving difficult to do.

"I know you've been busy harvesting the sap, but we've missed seeing you." His father enveloped him in a hug. "Michaela insisted I come out and check on you."

Adam took a step back and forced a smile. "You can tell her I'm fine, though I've been sick for the past week. That's why I haven't stopped by."

His father's brow narrowed in concern. "If we'd known you were sick we'd have come to help earlier. You've just been so insistent on handling things alone —"

"I know, and you were right."

"Never thought I'd hear you admit that." His father smiled and squeezed Adam's shoulder. "What about the sap?"

He glanced toward the maple grove, but there was no sign of Lidia or Koby. They must have taken the wagon, full of the morning's harvest, down to the sugarhouse.

Adam cleared his throat. "I've had some help."

His father leaned against the porch railing, a smile playing on his lips. "So you finally took my advice and hired workers?"

"Not officially." Adam's gaze dropped to study the rough boards of the porch. As much as he knew he needed to tell his father the truth, the very idea sent a wave of nausea coursing through him. "There is a problem, though. We need to talk."

"What is it, son?"

"Why don't you come inside and sit down. I'll get you some coffee."

He was avoiding the issue, and he knew it. He studied his father's puzzled expression as they entered the house. Adam wasn't sure how he did it, but the past year and a half had produced a deeper strength in his father. He'd seen the tragedy draw him and his stepmother, Michaela, even closer together as they rallied around the family for support. Their spiritual lives had taken on deeper meaning, but none of it made sense to Adam. It seemed to him that God had played favorites between Samuel and Jarek — and Samuel had lost.

"Something smells good." His father made himself at home on one of the two chairs Adam had to offer. "Don't tell me you've taken up cooking?"

"Hardly." He handed his father a mug of the hot coffee, then took a seat across from him. "I told you I've had some help. About a week ago I passed out in the snow and hit my head rather hard. Lidia Kowalski and her brother Koby were looking for shelter from the weather and stumbled, literally, upon me. They both work at one of the mills, but with the weather so unpredictable Lidia was afraid she wouldn't find her way back. I was in and out of consciousness, so she decided to stay and begin harvesting the sap."

"I wish we would have known. Thank God you're all right."

"I'm feeling fine now, and in fact I planned to take them back to the mill this morning so I could explain to the overseer what happened. I don't want them to lose their jobs over this. But . . ." Adam paused to take a sip of his coffee. "I found something out this morning about Lidia and Koby."

His father leaned forward, resting his elbows against his thighs. "What is it?"

Adam worked to formulate his words. There was simply no easy way around it. "Lidia's brother Jarek is the one who killed Samuel."

The color drained from his father's face. "How do you know this?"

"She was cleaning the room and found some newspaper articles I'd kept. She knew her brother was wanted for murder, but never knew who he'd killed until she saw Samuel's name. She put two and two together. . . ."

His father set his coffee on the small table beside him and rubbed his chin with his hand. "I'd given up ever knowing who had pulled the trigger, so much time has passed."

"Lidia has no idea where he is, but we have a name now, which will help. Knowing who it is means we might be able to narrow the scope of the search. They moved here from Boston, so it would make sense for him to go back to the place that is familiar to him."

"I suppose you're right, but what about Lidia? She must be quite upset."

"Of course she's upset, but so am I."

Adam marched across the room to the window before spinning around to face his father. "The last thing I want is for her to get hurt, but didn't you hear me? We know who killed Samuel, which means we can go after him and find him."

"It's been a year and a half. Sometimes I think it might be best if we simply let things go."

Adam raked his fingers though his hair, fighting the emotions that battled within him. "Answer this question. Why would God allow Samuel's life to be taken and let a murderer go free?"

"I know it doesn't make sense, and don't think I haven't asked myself the very same question a thousand times." His father pressed his palm against the smooth wooden arms of the chair. "All I know is that our God is not unjust. He might not work the way we want Him to, but that doesn't change who He is. Read through Romans chapter nine when you get a chance. It talks about God's sovereign choices toward man."

Stopping at the window, Adam's hands gripped the sill. He didn't want to hear about God having the right to be compassionate toward a murderer. He wanted answers. He wanted revenge.

The last days of winter were fading in

front of him. Already the changing weather had left dry patches on the ground, warmed by the morning sun. Before another week passed, his run of sap would be over. He wouldn't even have a harvest if it hadn't been for Lidia and her brother. He owed them everything, and yet all he could think about was the fact that their brother had destroyed Samuel's life. His father was right. He needed to put the past behind him and forgive, but putting one's words into action had proved to be nearly impossible.

His father stood and walked toward him. "I can't work through this for you, but you're going to have to come to terms with what happened if you ever plan to go on with your life. It wasn't Lidia's fault her brother took Samuel's life. And it's not your fault you couldn't stop it from happening."

Adam's stomach clenched. "It *is* my fault. Samuel shouldn't have died."

His father wrapped his arm around Adam's shoulder. "You have to stop blaming yourself. You're not responsible."

Adam stared out the window. Lidia walked beside her brother toward the maple grove. Her normal smile was missing. Instead her brow was furrowed with worry. Did she hurt as much as he did? He was a coward, but he couldn't face her again. At least not today.

He turned to his father. "Would you mind taking Lidia and her brother back to the mill? If there's any problem with them keeping their jobs, I'll make a trip out to talk to their overseer."

EIGHT

Lidia swung her leg over the thick branch of the elm tree and worked to untangle the rope that had caught on one of the limbs. More than likely, it was one of the Miller boys who managed to rig the seat of the swing so it hung lopsided, though none of the young neighbors would own up to the offense.

"Be careful, Miss Lidia."

Lidia looked toward the ground from her precarious position in the tree at Adam's younger sisters, Ruby and Anna Johnson. Only two adorable nine-year-olds would compel her to temporarily disregard all attempts at being a proper lady to scale the rough trunk of a backyard tree. Well, that and a rabid dog, she supposed, but at the moment, thankfully, she felt perfectly safe from any such threats. Something she hadn't felt for a long time.

It never ceased to amaze her how God

worked in such marvelous and mysterious ways. Adam once saved her life from a rabid mutt, and now his parents were doing the same thing. Not that her life was in danger now, but she still felt as if they had saved it. Instead of leaving Koby and her on their own to find jobs after Mrs. Moore dismissed them, Mr. and Mrs. Johnson had hired them to work on the Johnson farm.

Lidia untangled the rope, careful to keep her balance in the process as she teetered on the edge of the branch. She had no idea what Adam would think now that she was living on his parents' farm. She'd seen his face the day she rode away from his cabin with his father barely two weeks ago. The hurt in Adam's eyes had been clear, as though she'd betrayed him with the truth. He might have had feelings toward her at one time, but they had vanished with her confession.

She shook her head. Adam Johnson and his maple grove weren't her problems anymore. She refused to pine after a man who couldn't put the past behind him. She was dreadfully sorry for what her brother had done, but nothing she could ever say or do would change what had happened. The rest of the Johnson family, in giving her and her brother employment, had decided to move on with their lives. Something she could only hope and pray Adam would one day do, as well.

She gave the rope one more tug, and it broke loose. "All right, girls. I think it's fixed."

Dropping the rope, she watched the swing fall to its proper position. Pleased at her accomplishment and the giggles now emanating from the girls, she allowed herself a moment to enjoy the patchwork of rich earth that spread out before her. With spring clearly on its way, the acres of farmland were beginning to wake from their winter sleep. Soon mayflowers, hydrangeas, and a vast array of flowers would bloom. The apple orchards would begin to bear fruit. Pastures with their stone fence borders were dotted with grazing cattle, and in the distance the banks of the Connecticut River rose from the water.

Taking in a deep breath, she relished the fresh scent of spring that hovered in the air like a bee ready to take nectar from a blossom. It had been a long time since she'd felt so free and happy, and she had no intention of losing this feeling.

Dust rose in a hazy cloud to the north. A horse and rider galloped across the dirt road toward the Johnsons' house. Not wanting to be found in such an awkward position, Lidia began to make her descent. She felt a sudden tug at her waist. Reaching behind her back with one hand, she felt the material that had caught on one of the branches, but it was too taut for her to loosen it. She tried squirming free, but the fabric only pulled tighter. If she weren't careful she would rip a hole in the dress. With only three dresses to her name, she certainly couldn't afford ruining one of them.

"Hurry down, Miss Lidia. Adam's coming."

Lidia froze. Ruby and Anna jumped with excitement below her. For the first time all morning, Lidia regretted agreeing to watch the girls while their parents went into town. Surely she hadn't heard them correctly. Adam was supposed to be on his farm finishing the sap harvest. Not here. Not now. The girls continued squealing with delight as they watched their older brother and his black stallion approach the back of the gray-shingled farmhouse.

Her jaw tensed as he drew closer. He looked so handsome wearing Levis and a tailored work shirt with his Stetson pulled low across his forehead to block the sun's warming rays. He pulled on the reins as he approached the tree, then jumped off his horse, his eyes lighting up as his sisters enveloped him with their hugs, greeting him with more excitement than a fireworks display on the Fourth of July.

The wind ruffled his hair when he took his hat off, and she could see the shadow of stubble covering his jawline. This wasn't the Adam who kissed her in the moonlight beneath a blanket of stars. That man had vanished, taking with him a piece of her heart. She fought against the sense of panic that swept over her, not knowing what he would think when he realized she was hovering above him. She'd known he would show up eventually, but she planned to be ready to see him at that point. Not perched in the top of a tree with her skirt caught on a branch.

She tugged on her dress again, but the material wouldn't budge — and neither could she. Lidia closed her eyes. He hadn't noticed her yet. Maybe if she couldn't see him, he would disappear.

"Lidia?"

Facedown on the limb, she peeked through her lashes, her stomach feeling as if it were lodged in her throat. Adam shook his head, his eyes widening with surprise.

Oh Lord, how do I manage to get myself into such embarrassing situations? And just when I think I've finally got things in my life under control.

"Adam. Hello." Swallowing hard, she pulled on her dress again, but no matter what she did, it wouldn't release its grip.

He folded his arms across his chest and looked up at her. "If I remember correctly, this isn't the first time I've seen you in this position."

Lidia sighed. "It does seem that climbing trees has become somewhat of a habit for me, doesn't it?" *And a rather unladylike habit at that!*

"Are you coming down?"

She gnawed at her lip. "I can't."

"What do you mean you can't?"

Ruby jumped up on her brother's back, her arms firmly around his neck. "I think she's stuck."

"She was fixing our swing for us," Anna added, sitting on the wooden seat. "The Miller boys broke it."

"Is it true?"

Lidia tried to slow her quickened breathing. "That the Miller boys broke the swing?"

"No, that you're stuck."

"I'm afraid so." Lidia closed her mouth and tried not to let the irritation sweep over her. She could see the smirk that covered his face. "It's not funny, Adam."

"I'm sorry." He held up his hands. "I'm not making fun of you, it's just that . . ."

"That what?"

"Never mind." His smile melted into a solemn look. "Do I need to climb up and help you?"

"I think it might be necessary since I can't reach the spot where my skirt is caught without falling off the branch."

"Did you know you can see all the way to the Connecticut River on a clear day from there?" Adam set Ruby on the ground then easily shimmied up the trunk of the tree. "My brothers and I used to spend hours up here."

She tried to ignore the way the familiar sound of his voice pulled at her heart. Why did it have to be today, of all days, for Adam to decide to visit his family? She'd played out the moment in her mind a hundred times. He'd arrive at his parents' farm surprised to see her, but one look into her eyes and he'd realize that he'd been wrong. Nothing would stand between them and their future together. She shook her head. What had happened to her resolve to forget the man who couldn't forgive her? Daydreaming was going to get her nowhere except in trouble. At least where her heart was concerned.

Adam perched beside her on one of the branches and worked to unfasten the fabric. "I think this will fix things, and it's not even torn."

"Thank you."

Finally free, Lidia sat up. His face was only a few inches from hers, and her heart beat ferociously at his nearness. She was afraid to look at him, though, knowing she'd never again see the look of interest in his eyes that she'd once seen. Instead, she'd see the pain and know that her brother was responsible for putting it there.

Avoiding his gaze, she studied the intricate pattern of the bark and waited to follow his descent down the tree. As soon as he was on the ground, he reached up to help her. His arms encircled her waist. She was sure he could hear her heart as she worked to steady herself once her feet hit the grass. Raising her face toward his, she forced herself to look him in the eye. For a moment she found what she was looking for. They were back under the winter stars in his maple grove, before everything had gone so wrong. The world around her disappeared until it was only the two of them.

"Lidia, I . . ."

Her pulse quickened. "What is it?"

He took a step away from her and shook

his head. Whatever she'd seen in his eyes was gone. She could hear the girls playing again and feel the warm sun pressing against her face.

Anna sat in the swing while Ruby pushed from behind. Lidia tried to focus on the girls, but all she could see was Adam. In spite of what passed between them, she could feel the tension dissipate.

"The girls are happy. Why don't we talk?" He motioned her toward the back porch, no doubt wanting to converse in private as to why she was still here at his father's farm.

"All right." She matched his long stride, trying not to notice the strength of his profile. Instead she sent up a prayer that God would help him understand what she was about to say.

"I'm surprised to see you here." Adam stopped at the bottom step and leaned against the wooden railing. "I assumed because I didn't hear from you that everything was fine at the mill."

Lidia swallowed the lump that was growing in her throat.

"I don't know what you're going to think about this. . . ." Lidia fought to keep her composure. "When your father learned that my brother and I had lost our jobs at the mill, your parents decided to hire us both to help out on the farm."

Adam raked his fingers through his hair, not sure he'd heard Lidia correctly. "You're working for my parents?"

Lidia nodded. "The crop was so good last year that your father is planning to turn some of the pasture into additional fields, and with little Daria, your stepmother needed some extra help around the house —"

"My father never told me he was planning to expand his planting this spring or that he was hiring new workers." He shook his head, working to keep the anger out of his voice. Had he been so caught up with his own projects that he'd failed to listen to his father's plans? He was the eldest son. If his father needed help he should be the one filling in the gap. He would have found a way to make it work.

He kicked a pebble with the toe of his boot and watched the thin wisps of dust fill the air. When he'd first glanced up to see Lidia perched above him in the tree, he'd almost forgotten the last dark moments that had transpired between them. Instead the warmth of her kiss lingered in his memory, and with it the feelings he'd tried to forget.

But that wasn't enough. He appreciated

all that Lidia and her brother had done for him and admittedly owed them a lot, but how could his father consider hiring the siblings of the man who killed Samuel? He understood the need to forgive, but to go out of his way to give them jobs? It simply didn't make sense to him.

"I was afraid you'd be upset when you found out." Lidia's voice broke into his thoughts.

Upset didn't begin to describe his feelings. "My father . . . where is he?"

"He went into town with your stepmother. They asked me to watch the girls while they were gone."

He gripped the porch railing with his hand. "I don't understand. You lost your job at the mill? Why didn't you let me know? I would have gone and spoken to your overseer for you."

"It wouldn't have mattered. They'd already replaced us and made it clear that what we had done wasn't acceptable."

"I'm sorry. I . . ." He wasn't being fair to her, and he knew it. He should have stopped by the mill on his own accord.

She looked up at him with those big, brown eyes that were now rimmed with tears, and he cringed inside. When he'd watched her leave his farm with his father, he'd convinced himself that he could forget her. But now she stood before him even more beautiful than he remembered. Some of her hair had come undone from its braid, leaving auburn wisps of curls that framed her face. He didn't want to feel this way toward her — this attraction. No matter what feelings she invoked inside him, nothing would change the fact of who she was.

"And the harvest?" Lidia asked.

Adam raised his brow at her question. "I finished yesterday. I wanted to stop by and talk to my father about the sugaring off celebration. I haven't seen him since . . ."

"Since the day you found out my brother murdered Samuel."

"I guess there's nothing more for us to say then, is there?"

Lidia picked up the hem of her skirt and strode away from him, toward Ruby and Anna.

An hour later Adam felt his shoulder muscles burn as he swung the ax into the log behind the wooden shed on his father's property. The weather was still a bit chilly, but he was drenched in sweat.

His father rounded the corner of the structure and stopped beside him. "We'll have enough wood to last us until the turn of the century if you keep up this pace."

Adam threw the log onto the pile before plunging the blade into another thick piece of pine. "I wanted to talk to you before I went home."

"So your sisters said. Didn't expect to find you hiding out behind the shed, though."

"I'm not hiding."

"Then what is it?"

The blade cracked through the wood, splitting it down the middle. "I've been to the sheriff's office. I gave them the information I have on Samuel's killer."

"You mean Lidia's brother."

Adam wiped the moisture off his forehead with the back of his hand. "Why did you hire them?"

"They needed work, and I needed extra help around the farm."

"Don't make me feel guilty. I've tried to put the past behind me, but that doesn't mean I have to accept them into our family. For you to go and hire them . . ." Adam swung the blade to finish splitting the piece he was working on. "How could you even consider such a thing?"

His father tossed the fallen section onto the woodpile. "I don't understand your reaction, Adam. Lidia and her brother lost their livelihood because they helped you save your maple harvest."

"So now we owe them?"

"Yes! But I wasn't doing them a favor. Michaela and I had already decided we needed extra help around the farm. I want to expand this year, and with Daria taking up a lot of your stepmother's time, it seemed to be an answer from God that helped all of us."

"But why *them?*" The wood groaned as the blade forced it apart. "There are dozens of other people in town who could use the work."

"If you could forgive, you might be able to see that Lidia is a wonderful, godly woman."

"I know she's a wonderful person." The confession left an ache that radiated deep within him. That was the very reason why he had to stay away from her.

"I convinced the sheriff to raise the bounty on Jarek," Adam confessed.

"Why?"

Adam pounded the ax into the side of a stump. "Because I want him to pay for his crime."

His father took a step toward him. "And what about Lidia?"

"Her brother deserves justice."

"Yes, I suppose you're right, but how do you think she feels knowing that her brother will likely be sentenced to death?"

Adam shrugged, unable to answer.

"You're willing to lose Lidia?"

Adam cringed at the question. It was the very thing he was afraid of. That one day, he was going to regret just how much he'd lost in his search for justice.

NINE

Lidia let out a deep sigh of contentment as she watched the festive scene unfold before her from the Johnsons' front porch. The social gathering of friends and neighbors during the annual sugaring off had always been one of her favorite times of year. Laughter from the children mingled with the spirited sounds of a fiddle playing the chorus of yet another lively tune. Tonight's activities reminded her of good memories from the past with her family. And that God had blessed her with hope for a future again.

She watched Koby dip a paddle into the vat of maple syrup, then lick it clean. The grin on his face told her she had made the right decision in accepting the Johnsons' generous offer of employment. While she still considered herself merely one of the hired help, the Johnsons treated her as if she were a part of the family. It was a feeling she'd missed since the deaths of her parents.

"Are you enjoying yourself tonight?"

Lidia drew her gaze from the mesmerizing dance of the bonfire that crackled in the crisp night air and smiled at her new employer. "Very much, thank you, Mrs. Johnson."

It was hard to believe that Michaela Johnson would soon be a grandmother. Her eldest daughter, Rebecca Hutton, who now lived in Boston with her husband, had recently announced that she was expecting the Johnsons' first grandchild. Even with one-year-old Daria in tow, Mrs. Johnson always looked lovely with her pinned-up hair full of reddish highlights and her glowing fair skin. But it was more than her outward beauty that had impressed Lidia. It was what radiated from the inside — her contentment with life and generosity toward others as she managed a household of five children still living at home. Mrs. Johnson leaned against the rail beside her. "I was afraid it might be too cold, but it turned out to be perfect weather."

"Yes, ma'am, you're right." Lidia gazed at the cloudless sky. Above them, the stars glimmered in all their brilliance, covering the festivities in a canopy of lights. "I know

I've said it before, but I can't even begin to express to you how much it means to me and my brother that you and Mr. Johnson took us on. I know it couldn't have been easy, with what happened with Samuel —"

"That's not true." Mrs. Johnson laid a reassuring hand on Lidia's shoulder. "You've been an incredible help already. I must have told Eric a dozen times that I don't know what I'd do without you."

"Still, I do appreciate it."

Mrs. Johnson smoothed down the front of her lavender dress, its design simple, yet elegant — perfect for the festivities. "There's plenty of food and no excuses not to indulge tonight."

Lidia glanced at the wooden table that was laden with meats, salads, sandwiches, and doughnuts, as well as the customary pickles to counteract the sweetness of the syrup. "I promise to make myself a plate in a little bit. For now, I'm just enjoying watching all that's going on."

A short distance across the lawn, Adam walked up to the table and began filling his plate. Lidia felt her jaw muscles tense. So far she'd managed to avoid him, something she knew she wouldn't be able to do forever. Of course, more than likely he had no desire to see her either, but she refused to have her evening spoiled by him.

He looked up and his gaze swept past her, before returning to linger on her face. Her breath caught in her throat, and she wondered if she would ever forget him. But there was nothing in his eyes tonight that hinted that he still cared. Sadness filled his expression. Was he sorry that he'd changed his mind about calling on her? When he turned away without saying a word to her, the answer was clear.

Lidia turned back to Mrs. Johnson. "Why do you think Adam still hangs on to so much guilt regarding his brother's death? It wasn't his fault."

"And it wasn't your fault either, Lidia."

Her fingers gripped the wooden rail. "I know, but it's hard not to feel responsible. Jarek is my brother."

"I learned a long time ago that bitterness will only bring you pain and heartache. Adam has his own lessons to learn, but don't torture yourself over things you can't control."

"Still, I can't imagine how he must feel, and . . ." Lidia paused, not sure she should reveal her feelings toward Adam.

"What is it?"

"I don't know. I shouldn't even bring it up, but before Adam found out who I was he looked at me differently. Maybe nothing would have ever come from it, but there was something in his eyes. Sometimes I wish . . ."

"That he still cared for you."

Lidia nodded. "He was a complete gentleman while Koby and I were at his place, but one night . . . there was something romantic about the frosty air and the brilliance above. When I looked into his eyes, I knew he cared about me. He kissed me and told me he wanted to call on me once I was back at the mill. But all that changed when he found out the truth about my brother. Then nothing mattered anymore except that I was Jarek Kowalski's sister."

"I'm so sorry, Lidia." Mrs. Johnson turned toward Lidia, her eyes filled with concern. "Unfortunately, I don't think Adam even talks to his father much anymore. He's done a good job of closing himself off from people."

Lidia fingered the soft fabric of her skirt. "I'm praying he can someday put the past behind him and give me a chance, but I know that can never be."

"I wouldn't say that. Give him some time. Adam's a fine man who needs to deal with what happened, but we're praying there will come a day when he finally lets go of his guilt. Then he'll be ready for love."

"I'm not naive, Mrs. Johnson." Lidia shook her head. "Loving me would never be enough motivation for him to forgive Jarek."

"Don't be so sure about that. God has ways of bringing healing that we could never imagine. I'm always here for you if you need to talk. I know I can't take the place of your mother, but I can certainly be a friend."

Sensing the genuineness behind Mrs. Johnson's words, tears welled in Lidia's eyes. Things might never work out between her and Adam, but that didn't diminish the gratefulness she felt for God putting them together with this family.

Baby Daria cried from inside the house, and Mrs. Johnson moved toward the front door. "She was supposed to be asleep. If you'll excuse me —"

"You have guests." Lidia followed behind. "I don't mind checking on her."

"Are you sure?" Mrs. Johnson turned to her.

"It's no problem at all."

"Very well, then." A grin crossed the older woman's face. "I do need to check on Mr. Wentworth. Widow Sharp has her mark set for him, and last time I saw him, his face was as flushed as a ripe tomato."

Lidia laughed. In her short time on the farm, she'd heard of the Johnsons' nearby neighbor, Widow Sharp, who even at the age of eighty-two was determined to marry again despite the fact that she'd already buried four husbands.

"One more thing before you go inside." Mrs. Johnson grasped Lidia's hand and squeezed it gently. "You're a lovely young woman. I have no doubt that not only did God bring you into our family for a purpose but also that He has something, maybe even someone, very special in mind for you and your future."

Lidia wanted to believe her, but she had no illusions that life always ended happily ever after. Still, the Bible did promise that God could work all things together for good. All she could do was to pray that was exactly what He was doing.

Adam set his empty plate down on the table and scanned the lively crowd for Lidia. Social events like this made him want to get out his fishing pole and find a quiet spot away from it all. Having Lidia here made him even more uncomfortable. The sight of her talking to his stepmother earlier had caught him off guard. No matter how his emotions spun inside, he couldn't deny how beautiful she looked tonight. The pale green dress she wore, while modest, accentuated her figure and left him with an impulsive longing to gather her into his arms and kiss her once again beneath the silvery moonlight.

He didn't understand the intense draw he felt toward her. He knew plenty of pretty women, even beautiful ones, but they'd never caused his heart to race at such a rapid pace or his dreams to be constantly flooded with their presence.

Standing in the shadows beyond the reach of the light from the bonfire, he watched his sister Sarah's face light up with laughter as she ate another pickle. Sometimes it seemed that his own carefree days had vanished forever. Life had become all too serious. He missed the times when he had been able to laugh for no reason at all. When he didn't feel as if he carried the weight of the world on his shoulders.

Mr. Wentworth, with Widow Sharp on his arm, ambled in Adam's direction. Judging by the firm grip Widow Sharp had on Mr. Wentworth, there was no doubt that she had set her sights on yet another potential husband. Adam quickly slipped around the edge of the festivities and into the house. Perhaps he should have tried to rescue the timid farmer, but such attempts would no doubt do little to discourage Widow Sharp. And listening to her rambling talk of the weather and her seventeen grandchildren wasn't something Adam felt up to at the moment.

Inside, the house was quiet compared to the events going on outside. Everyone, it seemed, was content to enjoy the crisp night air and the festivities and food that went along with the annual sugaring off.

Away from the laughter and the serenade of the fiddle, a quiet lullaby reached his ears. Across the open living area, his littlest sister cooed contentedly, and he could see the silhouette of someone sitting in the rocking chair, gently lulling her back to sleep.

"Mother?"

The figure turned toward him. "Adam?"

A yellow glow from the crackling flames that radiated within the stone fireplace caught Lidia's profile and like a magnet drew him a step closer. "I . . . I didn't know you were in here."

The rhythmic sway of the rocking chair squeaked softly beneath her. "Daria was crying, and I told your stepmother I'd come check on her. I think she's about to drift off again, though with all the noise filtering in from outside, it's hard to believe she's able to sleep at all."

He shuffled his feet, the awkwardness growing between them, then cleared his throat. "Are you having a good time tonight?"

She ran her thumb across the back of the baby's head. "It brings back many good memories of when my parents were alive. The annual sugaring off was one of our favorite times of the year."

"Tell me about them." He perched on the edge of an upholstered stool across from her, thankful that the shadows of the room masked her expression. He was afraid of what he might find within the depths of her eyes.

"My parents?"

"You've told me about how they died, but there must be much to tell about how they lived."

The woodsy scent of the burning logs filled his lungs, as he stared into the yellow and orange flames. "Where we come from in Poland is very poor and overpopulated." Her voice sounded surprised at his question, but not as surprised as he was at himself for drawing out their conversation. "My parents were blessed to be literate, but the majority of my people are not. They saw this country as a place where they could give their children a better life. And not simply material things, but freedom." She paused a moment, as if she wasn't sure he really wanted to hear what she was saying.

"Go on. Please."

The creaking of the rocker slowed as she began to speak again. "My parents were hard workers who took whatever jobs they could find. While we lived in Boston, my mother worked as a seamstress, and my father, who had been a farmer in Poland, did everything from carpentry work to manual labor. They loved us, taught us to work hard, and put God first."

Lidia's voice quivered, and he wondered if she wasn't thinking of how her brother had rebelled against their parents' belief system. It must have hurt her family deeply to know what Jarek had done when all they'd wanted was a fresh start in life.

One of the logs burning in the fireplace popped, and Daria started crying. Lidia drew the toddler toward her and started singing again. Adam fidgeted with one of his cuffs as he listened to the sweet clarity of her voice.

His little sister took a deep breath and settled peacefully in Lidia's arms. If only Lidia didn't have an effect on him. Then his heart wouldn't have to wrestle with letting her go.

"I'd better leave." He stood quietly, not wanting to wake the child — or deal anymore with his own roiling emotions. "I need to go and find Ruby and Anna. I promised them I'd sample the syrup with them."

"Adam, wait."

He turned back around to face her.

"I know I have no right to say anything to you about what has happened between us, but I can't help it."

"Then don't, please." He couldn't bear to hear her say that she cared for him, because no matter what his own heart might feel, there would always be a wall between them. He didn't want to hurt her, but neither could he allow himself to continue something that he knew would never work.

Lidia shook her head. "This isn't about you and me, and what might have happened between us if the circumstances were different."

His jaw tensed. "Then what is it about?"

"It's about what happened between our families. It's about you getting on with your life and letting go of the bitterness you feel toward me, my brother . . . toward all of us. My people are no different from yours. While some of us make mistakes, all we

130

want is what is best for our families — political and religious freedom, and a place to call *home*."

At that he simply turned and left. His heels thudded against the wooden floor. He wanted to lash back at her, tell her that she was wrong. That he wasn't prejudiced toward her or her people, but in his heart he knew she was right. He longed to be the man God would have him be, but the emotions raging within him were like consuming fires as his conscience battled against the truth.

What would she think if she knew he'd talked to the sheriff about her brother? No doubt she'd feel betrayed. But he still believed he was right to seek justice for his family.

What if my desire for justice in turn ruins another family?

He cringed at the unwelcome thought and wondered when life had become so complicated. But there was more to the story than Lidia knew. More than anyone knew. That was why he couldn't let go of the past and be with Lidia. And why he would never forgive himself for what had really happened the day his brother Samuel was killed.

TEN

Adam pounded the last nail into the roof of the sugarhouse, then climbed back down the wooden ladder. Last night's storm had managed to loosen a number of the cedar shingles from both the sugarhouse and the roof of his cabin. Thankfully, the damage had been minimal, saving him from losing valuable time on more repairs.

Stepping off the last rung of the ladder, he paused to look out across his land. Winter's snow had melted away, leaving behind a green collage of ridges and valleys that blended into the woodlands in the distance. Besides the damage to the roofs and a few broken limbs, there were no obvious signs of the spring gale that had passed through overnight. Instead, the sun's rays bathed the land in its brilliant light.

He reached up to adjust the brim of his hat against its glare. His dreams for this farm went far beyond the sugar maple grove that stood in anticipation of next winter's harvest.

He had plans to expand the brick foundation of the house, adding extra rooms with hardwood floors and a large window to capture the view of the sloping hills that eventually led to the Connecticut River in the west.

To the east, he wanted to build a twelve-stall horse barn with a riding ring, as well as fenced-in pastures for cattle. With horses as the principal means of transport, breeding would ensure a steady source of income in addition to cultivating the rest of his acreage. Working the maple grove had given him his first real taste of what hard work could accomplish, and he knew he wanted more.

Already the crystallized blocks of maple sugar that would later be broken up or shaved had been poured into wooden molds, ready for the buyer who would arrive tomorrow. Glass syrup jugs were lined up, as well, filled to the top with the sweet liquid and ready to be sold in the surrounding stores all the way from Cranton to Springfield.

He had decided to give Lidia and her brother a portion of the profits, knowing if it weren't for their hard work he would have lost the majority of this year's harvest. While her financial standing had no doubt improved because of her new position on his parents' farm, he knew that the extra savings would help.

At the thought of her, Lidia's image flashed in front of him. Try as he might, he hadn't been able forget her. Seeing her face in the recesses of his mind reminded him of something else. What good were all his plans if he couldn't share them with someone? Was his anger and guilt worth the price of living alone? Without Lidia?

Hooking the ladder back on the wall of the sugarhouse, he bit back the questions. There were plenty of other women who would be more than willing to share a life with him. Two Sundays ago he'd been introduced to Silvia Dolny. From his short conversation with her, she had not only seemed to be intelligent but possessed a sense of humor, as well. She certainly wasn't lacking in good looks, either. Her hair was the color of honey, her complexion perfect . . . and not once had he thought of her until today.

Why hadn't it been that easy to forget Lidia . . . and the anger that separated them? Tool bucket in hand, Adam made his way back toward the house. Last night at the sugaring off, Lidia's pointed words had struck their mark somewhere deep inside him. Who was she to confront him when she knew little of what had really happened that day?

The wrath of man worketh not the righteousness of God.

The toe of his boot struck a rock, and he kicked it off the dirt path. He'd read the verse from James last night, knowing that he'd lived far too long wrapped up in his own anger and bitterness. He felt like Jacob who in the Old Testament had wrestled with God as he fought to lay aside his own anger, hurt, and guilt. Adam had lain awake half the night trying to come to terms with not only his own prejudices toward others but his guilt, as well.

He'd also read through the ninth chapter of Romans as his father had suggested. The passage had opened his eyes to another side of God's character. Paul said that God was not unjust, but instead, in order to make the riches of His glory known, He chose whom to be merciful to and whom to have compassion on. Had God, who saw beyond Adam's own human viewpoint, had a greater plan in mind when He chose not to save Samuel that day?

"Adam!"

Pulled from his heavy thoughts, Adam

glanced up the windy road that led into town. Thirteen-year-old Sarah drove the wagon toward him, sandwiched in between Ruby and Anna, who were bouncing in their seats. Living alone on the farm had taken time to get used to. The church he attended had blessed him with a number of friends, but hard work on the surrounding farms made socializing for many of them few and far during the busy times of the year. While he enjoyed the peace away from his younger siblings' squabbles, it was always a treat to have visitors — especially family.

Ruby clasped her hands together once Sarah had stopped the wagon in front of him. "We brought you something, Adam."

Adam swung Ruby down from the buckboard, then proceeded to help Anna. Sarah had already climbed down on the other side, a sly grin on her lips.

"It's a surprise." Anna jumped up and down, hardly able to contain her excitement.

Ruby grabbed both of his hands and spun him around. "Guess."

"Guess what?"

"What we have for you."

Sarah picked up a large basket, then joined them beside the wagon. The forlorn howl of a puppy sounded from the basket.

"No fair." Ruby stomped her feet. "Now you know."

"And all this time I'd thought you brought me lunch."

Sarah handed him the basket. "Be glad I didn't cook anything for you."

Adam laughed. Sarah was known in the family for her love of animals, not her domestic qualities.

Ruby leaned in beside him. "Daisy had puppies a few weeks ago, and we decided you needed one. No farmer can be without a dog."

Adam cautiously opened the lid, not sure of what he was in for. The yellow dog, with ears almost as big as his head, jumped up and licked him across the side of the face.

The girls broke out into a chorus of laughter.

"He likes you," Anna cooed.

"I don't know if I've got time for a puppy." Adam stared out across the open field waiting to be plowed and planted, but the grin never left his face.

"Of course you do." Ruby buried her face in the puppy's coat and wiggled her head as it continued licking.

"I thought puppies were a lot of work," Adam said. "And trouble."

"Only when they chew on Pa's shoes."

Adam ruffled Ruby's dark hair. "Sounds like words from experience."

The girls began to spew out their defense, sprinkled with words of advice for caring for a puppy.

"Hold on here." Adam took the puppy out of the basket and held it up in front of him. "I suppose we ought to come up with a name for him if I decide to keep him."

"What about Fluffy?"

"That's not bad." Adam mulled over Anna's idea. "He definitely is a ball of fur."

"What about Max?"

"Or Matilda."

"Matilda?" Adam choked back a laugh at Ruby's suggestion. "Reminds me more of someone's portly aunt than a puppy."

Anna reached up to scratch the dog's ear. "Lidia suggested Star. She adores puppies, just like we do."

Adam's jaw tensed. Had she remembered the night he kissed her under the stars when she suggested that name, or had she managed to put what had happened between them behind her? Judging from the admiration shining in Anna's brown eyes, Lidia had obviously captured the hearts of his family.

"Look at his back end." Ruby turned the dog around despite its nipping at her hand.

"There's a spot that looks like a little white star."

"It's a nice name," Sarah said. "I think you should pick that one."

Adam swallowed hard, wishing that he could forget Lidia but doubting that was possible. "Sounds like you've got a name then, Star. But you're not going to be any trouble now, are you?"

Star simply yipped, then proceeded to wet down the front of Adam's freshly laundered shirt.

Lidia closed her father's worn copy of *Nature* by Ralph Waldo Emerson and filled her lungs with the fresh spring air. With her regular morning chores complete in the house, Mrs. Johnson had insisted Lidia go outside to enjoy one of the season's first warm days until it was time to start preparing the evening meal. Glancing at the small watch pinned to her dress, she stood up quickly. She'd been so engrossed in the book, she hadn't realized how much time had passed, and the last thing she wanted to do was take advantage of her new employer's generosity. There was always plenty of ironing and washing needing to be done at the house, and frittering the day away wouldn't help to accomplish any of it.

Even though the distraction had been pleasant, it hadn't been enough to rid her of her thoughts of Adam. The girls had gone to his farm this morning to take him one of Daisy's new puppies and had insisted she join them for the excursion. The thought of seeing Adam again made her uneasy, so she had managed to find a way to persuade them to go without her.

She had, though, gone along with their naming game and threw out the first suggestion that came to mind. Star. It was true that the tiny ball of fur had a white star on his back, but there was a deeper meaning to the name. The brilliant stars shining overhead would always remind her of Adam and the night he kissed her.

There was another incident that continued to bother her. Last night at the sugaring off, she'd seen the look of torment in Adam's eyes. How she could have been so bold as to blatantly tell Adam he was prejudiced she had no idea. She only wanted to encourage him so he could find peace. No doubt her unladylike forwardness had done little good and instead had widened the gap between them.

She headed toward the house, the memory of Adam walking away from her still fresh in her mind. If only he knew that she'd never meant to hurt him. The past two weeks had shown her what true forgiveness was. She knew she didn't deserve the Johnsons' forgiveness over their son's death, let alone for them to hire her and Koby on as help. Yet they had gone beyond merely voicing their forgiveness. They had acted upon it.

This acceptance of her for who she was had made an imprint in her life that could never be erased. Claiming to be Christian was something she'd seen dozens of people profess. Actually living the life of one called to follow Christ had always been harder for her to find. It was something she had begun to pray that she could implement into her own life.

"Lidia?"

Sarah emerged from the barn with three of Daisy's puppies yipping at her heels. The sight of the frisky animals couldn't help but lighten her somber mood.

"They're adorable, aren't they?" Lidia shoved her book under her arm, then scooped up the little brown and white runt and began scratching him behind his ears.

Sarah shoved a loose piece of her blond hair out of her eyes and nodded. "I hate the fact that we have to give them all away, but my father would never allow for us to keep them all."

Lidia laughed as the puppy licked her chin. "Maybe he'll let you keep one."

"It is worth a try, but I know my father. As much as he loves animals, he believes firmly that they were made to help mankind, not the other way around." Sarah picked up one of the puppies. "At least I can visit Adam's puppy when I'm over there."

"What did Adam think about your present?"

Sarah's eyes sparkled with amusement. "While he probably won't ever admit it to me, I'm convinced he loved it."

"I'm glad." Lidia set the puppy back down, watching as it pulled at the black laces of her boot.

"Adam liked your suggestion and named him Star."

Had he thought of her at all when he agreed to the name? Lidia shook off the ridiculous thought. "The name did seem to fit the pup."

"I think Adam likes you —"

Lidia frowned at the comment. "I don't think so."

She'd heard of Sarah and even Rebecca's attempts to play matchmaker between her and their brother, but this was a game she had no intention of being a part of. She knew all too well that she would be the one who ended up hurt.

"Don't be so sure. There's something in his eyes when he says your name." Sarah let the pup nuzzle against her neck. "Despite his ornery side, he's really a wonderful person. Besides, I think it would horribly romantic if the two of you got together. Just think of the stories you could tell your grandchildren about how you met when he saved you from a rabid dog."

Lidia brushed an imaginary piece of lint off her skirt and took a step backwards. "I really need to get back to work. Your stepmother will think I'm shirking my duties."

Sarah frowned, then reached out her hand to touch Lidia's sleeve. "I didn't mean to upset you. I wouldn't have said anything if I didn't think you liked him, as well. I just thought . . ."

Lidia bit her lip. Had her emotions been that transparent? Except for her bold confession to Mrs. Johnson last night, she'd been careful to keep her feelings toward Adam to herself. "I think your brother is a very nice man who will make a fine husband for someone one day. But not for me."

"I'm sorry." Sarah's cheeks reddened to match the narrow trim of her dress. "I just want my brother to be happy, and you're perfect for him —"

"No, I'm the one who's sorry." Lidia pressed her fingers against her temple as a headache started to throb. "I didn't mean to snap at you. Your family has been so wonderful to my brother and me. I just know that because of what happened, there can never be anything between Adam and me."

"So you do care about him."

"I didn't say that . . . I . . . I don't know." One of the puppies nipped at her leg, and she shook her skirts to shoo him away.

"I just think if two people really care about each other, there has to be a way for them to work it out."

Lidia couldn't help but smile at Sarah. "You're an incurable romantic, aren't you?"

"Yes, and someday I'll find my own true love."

Lidia headed toward the house, wondering if there was any chance that Sarah and her stepmother could be right. It would be easy to dream that everything was going to turn out fine. Lidia's grandmother's stories had always had happy endings, but life had proved very different. She didn't blame God for the losses she'd experienced, but that didn't keep her from wondering why He didn't do anything to stop them.

144

She gave her head a shake. Dwelling on the past would never help. Instead, she was going to put everything she had into her work. Maybe someday she'd find the right man with whom she could spend the rest of her life, but for now she was determined to be content being exactly where God had placed her.

Mr. Johnson stood on the porch, his hands stuffed into his jeans' pockets. "Lidia, I wondered if you would come inside for a moment. Michaela and I need to speak with you."

"Yes, sir." Lidia's mouth went dry as she made her way into the house. She knew she'd been taking advantage of the Johnsons' generosity by enjoying her book outside all afternoon. After all they had done for her, she should have known better. Losing herself in a book was no excuse.

Mrs. Johnson entered the room from the kitchen. Despite the apron that she wore, there were several patches of flour sprinkled on the sleeves of her coffee-colored dress. "Lidia, please have a seat."

Lidia perched on the edge of the sofa determined to hold her composure whatever they might say. She could always try to find work in town or even at one of the other mills if worst came to worst.

Mr. Johnson sat down beside his wife and squeezed her hand. "I've just come back from town where I spoke to the sheriff about your brother."

Lidia's eyes widened. She hadn't even imagined that they wanted to talk to her about Jarek. Had her brother finally been caught? A lump began to form in her throat. For over a year she'd known that someday this moment would come, but even the tempered joy of being able to visit him in jail wasn't enough to take away the apprehension she felt. After what he had experienced, Jarek wouldn't be the same boy who used to play tag with her in the summertime and help her with her math homework.

And there was another distinct possibility, as well. If a trial came, the Johnson family would have to relive their son's death in court, opening old wounds. They wouldn't want her and Koby staying with them anymore. Forgiveness could only go so far.

Mrs. Johnson leaned forward and Lidia was surprised to see compassion in her eyes, not judgment. "We're so sorry to have to tell you this, Lidia, but Jarek was killed three days ago by a bounty hunter."

ELEVEN

Reuben Myers was not someone Adam wanted to mess with. The burly business-man jumped down from his wagon in front of Adam's place, his thick arms bulging at his sides. Thankfully, Reuben had become one of Adam's best customers.

"Afternoon, Adam." The man's voice bellowed in the crisp air.

"Good to see you, Reuben." Adam walked over to where he'd placed the sugar crates in neat stacks so they were ready to be loaded onto the man's wagon. "I think you'll be pleased with the quantity from this year's harvest."

Reuben eyed the season's production of sugar that Adam had laid out on half a dozen solid wooden containers. "Would love to see another year like 1860. Maple sugar production was at an all-time high that year, but at least the demand is still fairly strong."

"Good, because next year I'm planning to

expand the harvest even more."

"I'm assuming you've heard the news from town?" Reuben began hoisting one of the heavy crates of maple sugar blocks onto the wagon, while Adam followed suit.

"Haven't gotten away from the farm for the past few days. Things around here have been too busy."

Reuben rested his fists against his wide girth. "Hope you don't mind me being the one telling you then, but bounty hunters killed the man who shot your brother."

"What?" Adam dropped his load against the wagon's lowered tailgate.

"Clean through the heart, I heard. Just like he deserved."

Adam closed his eyes for a moment. Instead of feeling relief as he'd expected, all he could see was Lidia's face. No matter what her brother had done, Lidia had never stopped loving him. Wouldn't he feel the same in her place? Nothing one of his brothers or sisters would ever do could break the bond of family he felt with them.

"Adam?"

"Sorry, it's just that . . ." Adam shoved the crate into the wagon bed, then went to pick up the last load.

"I know it must be a relief. I keep telling the sheriff that they are going to have to start turning away them immigrants from coming into our country." The purple veins in Reuben's neck began to bulge. "I say we send them all back to where they come from."

The wrath of man worketh not the righteousness of God.

Adam stood still. Not long ago he would have made the same fiery speech that Reuben was making right now. But today all he could hear was the prejudiced ring that marked every word.

". . . should hang the lot if you ask me. What do you think about that?"

Adam swallowed hard. His attitude had been no different from men like Reuben who liked to spread their hatred to the rest of the town. Yet, he realized, Jesus came to earth to change all that. To make people think differently. Hadn't all mankind been offered redemption through Christ no matter who they were? German, Italian . . . Polish. Adam certainly wasn't perfect, and yet he'd claimed Christ's forgiveness. Because of his heavenly Father's great love, Christ's death on the cross now covered Adam's many sins.

Adam took a slow, deep breath. "Reuben —"

"I even told the sheriff that if we gathered

some of those men together and —"

"Reuben, thank you for telling me about Jarek, but I was wrong. It's time I forgave him for what he did and stopped blaming an entire people for one man's wrongdoing."

Reuben's laugh shook his bulky torso. "He can't accept your forgiveness now, Adam. If you've already forgotten, the man's dead."

Adam stared at the ground. "I know, and I'm sorry."

"You're sorry he's dead?" The man's eyes flashed with antagonism. "I never thought the day would come when you'd be defending these intruders that have come into our towns and —"

"I've heard enough, Reuben. Jarek Kowalski did a horrible thing, but he also left behind a younger sister and brother who have had to struggle to support themselves —"

"Isn't that the exact point I've been trying to make?" Reuben grasped the edge of the wagon with one hand. "Life would have been better off for all of us if they'd never left their mother country in the first place."

It was no use and Adam knew it. Adam hoisted the final crate into the wagon bed, then slammed the wooden tailgate shut.

He avoided the older man's penetrating gaze. "I'll expect the second half of the payment in full by the end of the month," Adam said.

"You'll get it." The irritation that laced Reuben's words was impossible to miss. "I don't understand what's come over you. Of all the people involved, I assumed you'd regret not being the one to tie a noose around that murderer's neck. In the least be thankful someone else did it for you."

Adam straightened his back and stood tall. "I was, until I took a look at my own life and realized I wasn't any better than he was."

"You're a fool, Adam Johnson, if you believe that. Nothing more than a fool."

With a sullen shake of his head, the man climbed into his wagon and drove off. Adam sat down on a stump and rested his elbows against his thighs. He wanted to pray but wondered if God would even want to listen to him. How had it come to this?

There was no arguing the fact that his brother's death had been a violent wrongdoing, a horrid crime that could never be undone. Nor could the pain of that night ever be erased. But he'd let that one violent act completely change him. Bitterness had become a poison in his veins that had spread into his relationships with his family, with friends . . . and with Lidia. What kind of man allowed the ruthless acts of another to overcome every aspect of his being? He'd ended up no better off than the criminal who'd wronged him.

Adam combed his fingers through his hair. "God, I don't even know where to begin. How can I come before You, the Maker of this universe, when I don't even deserve another breath of air?"

The sky loomed above him as darkness began to settle across the wide expanse. Minutes slowly passed, but he didn't move from the stump. One by one, the stars made their nightly appearance, lighting up the sky like a million fireflies. It was a testimony of God's power. He had no doubt that the heavens — and all of creation — were proof of God's existence.

The heavens declare the glory of God; and the firmament sheweth his handiwork.

Adam felt small as the words from Psalms spun through his mind. The glory of God's universe surrounded him completely. Everything God had created was for a purpose. The sun, moon, and stars gave light to the earth. The nearby stream that trickled in the night air gave life to the vegetation. The maple trees that reached toward the heavens beside him were full of intricacies he would never completely understand. Yet he knew how to watch the gradual changes in the seasons and wait for the right temperature that would in turn give him the sought-after liquid from its depths.

It was one thing, though, to believe that he had a Creator. But the reality that the Maker of this world had sent His only Son to pay the ransom for Adam's sin was more than he could grasp.

His hands clenched together. "You knew the choices I would face from birth, God, yet I know I've failed You. How could You still love me enough to sacrifice Your Son for someone as worthless as I am?"

Because I chose you from the beginning. You're mine and I love you.

Adam froze. The words whispered quietly into the recesses of his mind shook him to the core of his being. How could his Creator truly love him?

I have chosen you and you are Mine. I love you.

Adam wanted to cry out at the repeated words. To scream that he didn't deserve God's love . . . Instead they began to wash over him like a healing balm.

"Forgive me, Lord." He fell face down onto the ground. Dust blew into his nostrils as he pulled his hands across the loose dirt.

"I want to be a man who can persevere in the face of trials and come out stronger because of them. I want to be a man who keeps his faith no matter what happens around me."

An unexpected peace began to envelop him. He might have stumbled through the fires of this trial and made a mountain of mistakes along the way, but his God had forgiven him. It was a forgiveness he didn't deserve — no one did — yet God offered it freely to anyone who would accept His unfailing love and follow Him. Strange how he'd heard sermons preaching the same lesson dozens of times since he was a boy, and yet it had taken this long for the words to pierce his heart.

Star ran up beside him and licked the back of Adam's neck. He sat up and rubbed the mutt's ears. "How are ya doing, boy?"

In spite of the seriousness of the moment, Adam laughed out loud. God must have a sense of humor.

"I guess God created you for a reason, as well, you little rascal." He gathered the pup into his arms. "While it might be hard for me to admit it, I've enjoyed your company. Especially the fact that you listen and never argue with me."

Emotionally drained, Adam felt a wave of

fatigue overcome him, but he knew that there was something left he had to do. He'd finally found it within himself to forgive Jarek for what he had done to his brother. Forgiving himself for what happened that day was something he knew he'd continue to struggle with, but come daybreak he'd head out to his parents' house. It was time to ask Lidia for her forgiveness.

Lidia stood on the front porch of the Johnson family home and watched the stars dance in the heavens above her. Since a girl, she'd been mesmerized by the beauty of the night sky. Like precious pearls strung out across a velvet mantle, they left her to wonder about what lay beyond Earth's landscape. Discoveries, like Maria Mitchell's finding of a new comet, or Asaph Hall's more recent detection of two satellites circling the planet Mars, had always fascinated her. Tonight, though, it was hard for her to find the beauty in anything around her.

Jarek was dead.

Somewhere, deep inside her, she'd managed to hold onto the sliver of hope that things would turn out differently. That all of this would be nothing more than a horrible mistake. That Jarek really hadn't killed Samuel, and any day now he was going to come riding back into her life as the boy she used to know.

But none of that would ever happen.

She'd never again watch Jarek play baseball in the dusty field behind her parents' row home. Never see his eyes light up when he laughed or pulled a childish prank on her or Koby.

Shivering at a gust of wind that swept across the open land before her, Lidia pulled her shawl closer around her shoulders and went inside the house. The living area was empty, though she could hear ripples of laughter coming from the lighted kitchen. The normally pleasant scents of cinnamon, brown sugar, and homemade bread wafted into the dimly lit living room, but tonight it only made her stomach churn. Food was the last thing she was interested in. Picking up a newspaper, she sat on the rocking chair beside the fireplace and creased the paper's folded edges.

The smoky light from the lantern that lay on the mantel above her fell across the page as Lidia thumbed through. She had no interest at the moment in editorials or fashion advice. A fancy dress to "sweep him off his feet" as the article promised would do nothing to bring back her brother. About to set the paper on the hearth, a small notice on the back page caught her eye.

Wife Wanted

Decent hardworking rancher is looking for a good Christian woman to join me on my large homestead in New Mexico. No drinkers or smokers. Seeking companionship and help on ranch. Suitable candidates please respond to the following address. Sincerely, Jonathan Washington Smith

Lidia ran her finger across the newsprint. She'd glanced at similar ads in the personals column of newspapers and never given them another thought besides wondering what kind of desperate woman would have the nerve to answer them.

Now she knew.

For the first time in her life, agreeing to marry someone she'd never met seemed far from ridiculous. In fact, it just might be the answer to her prayers — a way to completely start over. Laughter rang out from the kitchen, but she ignored the happy sounds. Surely she could find a good man who was in need of a faithful companion and who would be willing to take in her brother, as well. As long as he was treated kindly, Koby would earn his keep.

Pulling the paper to her chest, Lidia let out a deep sigh. How exactly did such an arrangement work? A short courtship by correspondence followed by a loveless proposal? The thought was far from appealing. Her childish dreams of her romantic champion coming to her rescue, falling in love, then living happily ever after would have to be forgotten. Romance wouldn't be a factor in such a formal transaction.

But what other option did she have? What would the people of Cranton think now that they knew her brother had murdered one of their own? No, she had no option but to leave, and while the very idea made her sick to her stomach, becoming a mail-order bride did hold a solution.

Engrossed in her thoughts, Lidia started as someone entered the room.

"Hello." Michaela dipped her head to gaze into Lidia's eyes. "How are you doing?"

Lidia shrugged her shoulders. Michaela handed her a plate with a gooey cinnamon roll, then sat on the brick hearth across from her. "I need your expert opinion. How is it?"

The newspaper slid to the floor as Lidia forced herself to take a small bite. "It's wonderful as always."

Michaela reached out to pick up the fallen paper, then balanced it on her knees. "I was afraid I might have added too much brown sugar this time."

Lidia couldn't help but reveal the hint of a smile at the comment. Michaela had already found out that brown sugar was one of her weaknesses. "That, as you know, would be impossible."

"Are you all right?" Michaela leaned forward, and the light from the lantern captured the reddish highlights in her hair.

"I will be."

"Let me know if you need anything. I'm here for you. We all are."

"Thank you." The reassurances from her employer helped, but they still weren't enough to bring Jarek back.

Michaela glanced at the paper, a puzzled furrow lining her brow. She held the paper up in front of her. "Don't tell me you've been reading advertisements for mail-order brides."

"I . . ."

What could Lidia say? She wouldn't lie, and yet such an admission would only hurt Michaela and her family if they knew that not only had she been reading them but also seriously considering such an option.

When did life get so complicated, God, that

I've begun to see the benefits in becoming a mail-order bride?

Lidia chewed on her bottom lip. "I've always thought them quite . . . amusing."

That was true, at least.

Michaela reached up to tame a curl that had escaped the confines of her hairpins. "My best friend, Caroline, and I used to read these every week, trying to read between the lines."

"What do you mean, read between the lines?" Lidia set the plate in her lap, unable to take another bite of the sweet bread, no matter how delicious it might be.

"Think about it." She tapped her fingernails against the paper. "A man, or woman for that matter, can say anything they want in a personal advertisement or letter. For all you know, Mr. . . ." She glanced again at the wording. "Mr. Smith is twice your age and lives in a run-down shack in the middle of the scorching New Mexico desert."

"How do you know —" Lidia choked out a laugh at the realization. "That's reading between the lines?"

Michaela nodded. "And no doubt he wants companionship, but more than likely he wants someone to cook his dinner and wash his clothes."

"Slop the pigs and can vegetables?"

160

Michaela's grin widened. "You're getting the picture."

"I don't know." Lidia shrugged a shoulder and let her fingers play with a loose thread on her skirt. "Jonathan Washington Smith . . . it's a nice name. He might really live on a huge ranch and simply be lonely —"

"And you might simply be trying to run away from your problems."

The truth hit hard. "My brother's dead, and I know people aren't saying good things about him . . . about me and Koby."

"It's not fair, is it?" Michaela rested her hand on Lidia's shoulder and caught her gaze. "There will always be those who find reasons to look down on others. I know how bad it hurts to lose someone you love so much, no matter what the circumstances. I've had my times of grieving, and it was never easy. Cry, scream, do whatever you need to do, but don't run away from the people who love you and care about you."

Lidia felt the tears begin to swell in the corners of her eyes. "I don't know if I can stay."

"Listen." Michaela reached out and gripped Lidia's hand as Koby's distinct laugh rang out from the kitchen, filling the recesses of her heart. "Your brother's thriving, and both of you are surrounded by people who love you like family. Don't throw it all away because you're afraid of what tomorrow might bring.

"Let God's Spirit work within you to bring you the strength you need for today. Then let Him help you again tomorrow and the next day. You can't do it alone, Lidia, and I can promise you that Jonathan Washington Smith doesn't care for you the way our family does."

Lidia squeezed her eyes shut to stop the flow of tears. She crinkled the edge of the paper and bit her lip. She understood Mrs. Johnson's concerns that answering an advertisement for a mail-order bride might not be the solution to her situation, but surely it wouldn't hurt to write Mr. Smith a letter.

Twelve

Adam rounded the bend of the road that led to the Johnson farmhouse and let the warm spring air fill his lungs. The wagon jostled beneath him as he followed the uneven lane past lush farmland that spread out beyond a row of towering pines. Evidence of the new season was noticeable wherever he looked. Grazing cattle wandered throughout green pastures, content to feed off the land's rich substance. Before long, a brilliant display of flowers would be in bloom, from the white blossoms of the hydrangea bush to the colorful rhododendrons that edged his parents' home.

The gray-shingled farmhouse, with its large front porch, came into view. Adam pulled on the reins to slow the horses' gait. This was the home where he'd been born and where he'd watched his brothers and sisters grow up beside him. Memories of afternoon baseball games, picnics, and church socials filtered through his mind. Those happy memories, though, were paired with vivid images of his mother's death and the emptiness he'd felt knowing she'd never be there to help him with his schoolwork or kiss him good night. Sometimes the memories still left a hole in his heart. Michaela's unexpected entrance into their lives had helped to draw him out, but life didn't stay static for long. It had hit him with one more punch. No one had expected Samuel to die so young.

The sun brought out trickles of moisture across the back of his neck, and he reached up to wipe them away, wishing he could just as easily wipe away his melancholy mood. Life wasn't always fair — he'd discovered that early on. But he'd learned an even greater lesson lately. God saw beyond the outer surface of a man. He saw into the very heart. But having the willing heart that God wanted wasn't always easy.

Drawing in the reins, he stopped the wagon in front of the house and jumped down. The yard was quiet except for a plump hen that had somehow managed to escape the confines of her coop. Even her annoying squawking wasn't enough to distract him from the real purpose of his visit. Adam's heart throbbed at the thought of seeing Lidia again. The last time they'd been together he'd been nothing like the gentleman he should have been and far from the Christian example he yearned to be. He could never make up for his actions. Just like he would never be able to make up for the pain she was feeling over her brother's death. That was one thing they had in common. They both understood the deep pain of loss. It might not ever bring them together as he'd once hoped, but it might help erase some of the uneasiness between them.

Reaching into the bed of the wagon, he pulled out a small basket he'd secured on the side. He'd brought Lidia a peace offering. He couldn't help but wonder what her reaction would be to seeing him again. Hopefully between the jar of maple syrup and his heartfelt words of apology she'd find it within her to forgive him.

Michaela walked out of the house with baby Daria partly hidden in the folds of her skirt. God had known what He was doing when He brought his stepmother from Boston to Cranton. She could never completely take the place of the mother he lost, but there had never been any doubt of her love for him or any of the other Johnson children.

"It's been too long since we've seen you." Michaela leaned against the porch railing. "Your father was starting to worry that maybe you were sick again."

Adam shook his head and smiled as he took the stairs two at a time, then embraced his stepmother with a warm hug. "Nothing of the sort. Just needed some time to come to my senses is all."

He pulled a shiny red ribbon out of his pocket for the dark-eyed toddler. Daria might be shy, but Adam found that a treat every now and again went a long way in gaining her affections. He tousled the child's hair, watching in amazement as she manipulated the shiny fabric between her fingers, her eyes lit up with joy.

"I've come to talk to Lidia." Adam cleared his throat. "I need to apologize to her. Blaming her for Samuel's death was wrong."

Michaela raised her brow. "What changed your mind?"

"I was forced to look at my own life and realize I wasn't any better than Jarek."

"That's a powerful conclusion to come to." Daria started to whimper, and her mother lifted the child onto her hip. "There's . . . there's something else you should know."

Michaela glanced away, and Adam's heart

skipped a beat. If something had happened to Lidia . . .

His stepmother pulled Daria against her chest as if trying to shelter the young child from the expected ups and downs she would face throughout her lifetime. "Lidia's brother was killed by bounty hunters a few days ago."

Adam let out a sigh of relief. "I know. Reuben Myers told me yesterday when he came to pick up his load of sugar."

A frown spread across her face. "I'm sure I wouldn't like to hear what he had to say about it."

"No, you wouldn't, but listening to him made me see what a fool I've been."

"Lidia's taken it hard. I'm pretty sure she thinks the town, and maybe even our own family, are going to turn against her now that they know it was her brother who killed Samuel."

Adam's gaze swept the sanded boards of the porch, and his stomach knotted together. "I was one of those people."

"And now?"

"I once blamed her for Samuel's death simply because they were kin. Now I realize how hatred and bitterness can affect the truth."

"You're right, but that still doesn't change

how she feels, or how she believes people see her." Michaela gently rocked the young girl who looked almost asleep against her shoulder. "I hope you can make things right with her and help her see that what happened doesn't change the way any of us feel toward her."

Still pondering his stepmother's words, Adam made his way through the farmhouse toward the backyard where Lidia was hanging out the laundry. Stepping into the kitchen's outer doorway, he stopped at the sight of her. The fabric of her beige dress billowed in the morning breeze as she reached up to secure a white sheet to the line. She'd gained some weight, which only accented her gentle curves. Several tendrils of her long auburn hair spilled across her shoulders, and the sun reflected a bit of color on her fair cheeks.

He couldn't deny the truth. From the very first moment he'd found her treed by that rabid dog, something within him had known that in meeting her, his life would change forever. In many ways it had. She'd shown him what real sacrifice meant, and what it meant to truly love one's fellow man.

Then there had been their kiss beneath the stars —

"Adam?"

The sound of her voice startled him.

"Lidia . . . I —" He stopped, suddenly uncertain of what to say.

"Did you need something?" Her voice rang cold and void of any emotion.

"I came to see you," he started again. "How have you been? I mean, I'm sorry. I'm sorry for . . ."

He stepped outside and hurried down the stairs, closing the distance between them so he could look into her eyes. He hated the sadness he saw in their depths.

She held her head high. "Sorry for what?"

"For everything." *Give me the words, Lord. Please.* "I'm sorry for the loss of your brother."

He had to start somewhere, but he wasn't sure he'd chosen the right place. Her eyes misted over, and she turned away from him, grabbing the next sheet from the basket in a quick, jerky movement as she flung it over the line.

Adam swallowed hard. "I know how much it hurts to lose someone you love."

Her gaze avoided his. "I thought you'd be happy now that your brother's murderer has paid with his life for his deed."

Her words pierced like a poisoned arrow to his heart. "I might have been — would have been — a few weeks ago, but not today."

"What's changed?" She kept her back to him.

This wasn't going the way he'd planned at all.

"Everything's changed for me, Lidia." He came around to the other side of the clothesline to face her. "When I see what you've gone through, it —"

"You don't have a clue what I've gone through." She flung a clothespin at him and struck him on the forehead.

Adam took a step back, not sure how to react to her display of emotion. "That's not what I meant."

Another wooden pin bounced off his shoulder.

Deciding he had nothing to lose, he set the jar of maple syrup down on the grass and continued, "Lidia, I've seen how you respond to life in a godly way no matter what happens. That's what you've taught me."

He ducked at the third clothespin. *Okay, maybe not in every instance.*

She looked up and caught his gaze. He expected to see anger in her eyes, but all that was left was pain.

"Lidia, don't you see? I've been so

blinded. You've shown me what true sacrifice is, and what it means to love someone through God's eyes."

Her head bowed and her shoulders shook as sobs racked her body. Adam moved toward her and gently took her hands, drawing them toward his chest. "I'm sorry, Lidia, for everything. I'm sorry your brother died, and I'm sorry I treated you the way I did."

Lidia leaned into his chest as he wrapped his arms around her.

This is where you belong, Lidia.

With his arms still around her, he led her to the porch stairs where they could sit down. She wiped her face with the back of her hands, before looking up and searching his eyes.

"I'm sorry about the clothespins."

He stifled a laugh. "I knew you had a bit of spunk in you, but I never imagined I'd have to defend myself from a fleet of flying clothespins."

A smile formed beneath her rounded eyes, and Adam felt his heart pound within his chest. No. Now wasn't the time for him to express his feelings toward her. Lidia had just suffered a horrible loss. He needed to be there for her without any hint of an ulterior motive.

And there was something else he had to do.

"I need to ask for your forgiveness." He tilted her chin so she couldn't look away from him. "I've let bitterness over Samuel's death run my thoughts and emotions. Not only did I blame your brother for what he did, I blamed you, Koby, and anyone else who got in my way."

Adam paused, trying to find the right words to say. "I . . . I guess there's nothing else I can really say, except that I'm sorry."

Lidia drew in a deep breath, her mind spinning at Adam's confession. She'd waited for so long to bridge the gap that hung between them. Their kiss had stirred something within her she'd never felt before, but she'd finally realized that any hope of a relationship between them had long passed. Saying sorry would never change that.

She laced her fingers together, trying to ignore the effect his nearness had on her. "Your reaction was no different than the dozens of other people in town who won't want anything to do with me once they find out that Jarek was my brother. You, of all people, had an even greater motivation. Samuel was your brother."

"That's no excuse." Adam shook his head

and rested his forearms on his thighs. "Not that I didn't have the right to be angry and hurt over what happened, but the way I acted was no better than Reuben Myers and his blatant hatred for immigrants. As for the rest of the town, most of them are good, upright people. I don't see them blaming you for what your brother did."

She leaned away from him. "Don't try to sugarcoat things for me, Adam. I've lived in this country long enough to recognize the expression on people's faces once they hear my last name. I've tried so hard to be an *American,* but no matter what I'm still an immigrant. At least to everyone else I am."

Shoving her hand into the pocket of her dress, she fingered the folded letter she'd written to Mr. Jonathan Washington Smith. This morning it had seemed to be the only way she could escape to a place that would take her away from all of this. She looked out across the land, past the newly tilled garden and toward the orchards and pasturelands. There would never be any escape from who she was.

Lidia Kowalski.

She couldn't deny it. Polish blood ran through her veins. Grandmother had always taught her to be proud of her heritage and who she was. Besides the Bible, her sweet babcia had charged her to remember the stories from her mother country. Stories she could in turn pass down to her grandchildren. In the end she'd betrayed her grandmother by trying to hide who she was.

I'm sorry, Grandmother. In betraying who I am, I've betrayed you . . . and Mother and Father. I've betrayed my very existence.

Crumpling the soft fabric of her skirt between her fingers, she looked up at Adam. "I always thought if I could talk like a lady without any accent no one would know who I really was, and I'd be accepted. I constantly corrected Koby over his grammar, and for myself, I read everything I could get my hands on so no one could ever accuse me of being ignorant. But I was wrong."

Adam leaned back against the porch rail. "There's nothing wrong with trying to improve one's self."

"But that wasn't my reasoning. I was trying to become someone I never could be. There's nothing I can do to change who I am. Nor should I ever want to." She held her head up high. "I'm an American *and* I'm Polish, Adam Johnson. It's time I started to be proud of who I am."

A deep feeling of peace flooded through Lidia's heart. Like cool, healing waters, it ran into the tiny holes and crevices that had been chipped away like broken pieces of pottery. For a moment, she sat still beneath the warmth of the morning sun, working to push aside the pain from her past.

Adam broke the silence. "You never answered my question."

She raised her gaze to meet his. "What question?"

"I need you to forgive me, Lidia. I'm not sure I'll ever be able to forgive myself, but I need to hear it from you."

Something stirred within her. It was like the first time she met him. For a brief moment she'd stood in the shelter of his arms knowing he was the one who'd rescued her from the rabid dog. Today his coal-black hair glistened in the sunlight. The gold glints in his eyes seemed to plead with her to forgive him.

"I do forgive you. What my brother did was horrible, but that still doesn't change the fact that I . . ."

"You what?"

Tears glistened in the corners of her eyes. "I miss Jarek so much. I know what he did was wrong, but . . . I can't help it. He was my brother."

"You have every right to miss him."

A strand of her hair blew across his face, and he pulled her closer. "I've forgiven your brother for what he did to Samuel."

"I wish he could have heard your confession, but at least I have —"

"Lidia!"

Lidia turned to see Koby running toward her at full speed. "What it is, Koby?"

"Aren't you ready to go yet? The wagon's loaded."

She lifted her fingers to her mouth. "I'd entirely forgotten."

Adam turned to Lidia. "Forgotten what?"

"We're supposed to go to a barn raising for the Nowaks. They're a Polish family who live nearby."

"I suppose I'd better go then." Adam stood, shoving his hands into his pockets. "I have plenty of work to do on the farm —"

"Why don't you come along, Mr. Johnson?" Koby piped up. "Your entire family's going, and the food's going to be wonderful. Hunter's stew, noodles and cabbage, cucumber beet soup —"

"Cucumber beet soup?" Adam wrinkled his nose.

"Come on. It will be fun."

Lidia saw a flicker of hesitation register in Adam's eyes. Did he wish that they could prolong their time together? Did she? Despite all that had transpired between them, she couldn't ignore that her heart didn't want things to end this way. Still, sharing a kiss beneath a starlit sky didn't promise them a future together. Just like asking for one's forgiveness didn't erase the pain. Adam might feel bad about the way he had treated her, but so much heartache had transpired between them. Nothing could ever change that fact.

"Please come," Koby begged.

"Would you mind, Lidia?" Adam shifted uncomfortably beside her.

Her breath caught in her throat. She couldn't determine if she was more nervous or excited with the opportunity to prolong their time together. "Of course not."

"I'm not much on socials, and I don't promise to try any beets . . ."

Koby laughed. "Then, if we're all going, we'd better hurry."

Lidia followed them into the house and tried to untangle the web of confusion she felt tugging at her. Part of her longed for Adam to acknowledge that he cared for her. Another part wanted to run away and forget that she'd ever met him.

I don't know what to do anymore, Lord. Please, show me Your will for my life.

Stopping at the threshold of the living area, Lidia reached into her pocket and fingered the one-page letter she'd written to

Mr. Smith. The thin paper crinkled between her fingers. All she had to do was send it in the mail, and if Mr. Smith agreed, she and Koby could be on the next train to New Mexico. Surely she and Mr. Smith would be able to find a way to make a marriage work.

If that was true, though, then why was her heart begging her to stay?

THIRTEEN

Lidia watched Koby mingle with a group of friends on the other side of the newly constructed barn. He was eating a plate of noodles and cabbage and laughing as if the world were free from any cares.

Adam, on the other hand, stood beside Lidia looking uncomfortable in his starched white shirt and black pants. He seemed to have enjoyed working with the other men during the barn raising, but now that the celebration had begun, he'd grown quiet and reserved. Standing rigid, he pulled at his collar, then shoved his hands into his pockets. He didn't have to say anything for her to recognize that he felt like a frog in a bees' nest.

The structure bustled with activity around them. A dozen couples stomped their feet on the rough wooden floor in the center of the barn as they danced to a Polish folk song played by a group of fiddlers. The vivid colors of the women's skirts swished before her, while smells of sawdust mingling with savory meats filled the air.

Lidia looked up at Adam, her hands behind her back. "Are you sorry you came?"

"Of course not." He tugged on his collar again and chuckled. "Though to be perfectly truthful, I could have done without the beet soup."

Lidia laughed. He'd finished off two bowls of Hunter's stew with relish but had sampled the cucumber beet soup under protest. "I don't suppose it's a crime to dislike beets."

"I hope not. I've always tried to avoid that and squash."

She smiled, reminded of what she liked about him. He might not be one for social gatherings, but he was handsome, honest, and he made her laugh.

"I hate liver and cooked spinach," she confessed, enjoying the festive spirit around her and the growing camaraderie between them. Only a few short hours ago, she'd been ready to take the next train out West in reply to Mr. Smith's advertisement. But with Adam standing beside her, she felt the now familiar tugging of her heart begging her to stay and at least see what might happen, if anything, between them.

The fiddlers stomped their feet and picked up the tempo a notch. Lidia loved celebrations like today. The music lifted her spirits and set her heart soaring. If she closed her eyes, she could imagine her father's wide hand on the bow of the violin and her mother's smile as she swayed to the music from Poland.

Jarek's image flashed before her.

Jarek murdering Samuel . . . His face on the wanted poster . . . Jarek running from the law . . . Jarek killed at the hands of a bounty hunter . . .

Guilt overwhelmed her.

I shouldn't be here, Lord. I shouldn't be smiling. There's too much pain to laugh again.

The music closed in around her, but this time the beauty had vanished. The room moved in slow motion. Someone laughed. Voices buzzed in the background.

It's time to turn your mourning into dancing.

Lidia gripped the edge of the wooden table beside her and attempted to keep her balance. How many times had she prayed that God would turn her sorrow into joy? That she would hear laughter once again in Koby's voice? That she would be able to dance with joy?

Dance, Lidia. Dance for joy, for I will make you whole again.

"Lidia. Are you all right?" Adam's fingers brushed her elbow.

She stared up at him. "I don't know."

Another song started, and her foot tapped automatically to the familiar rhythm.

"Let's dance." Lidia blurted out the words before realizing how forward she sounded, but for once she didn't care. "It's a traditional *mazurka* from Poland. You'll be able to catch on —"

"No, I'm sorry. . . ." He took a step backward. "I can't. I'm sorry. . . . I'm not much for dancing."

Lidia swallowed her disappointment.

I came to set you free, Lidia. Dance for joy!

She glanced up at Adam, who gave her a weak smile. Lidia stepped out onto the floor with the other dancers and quickly chose a partner. She let the music fill her senses, her heart racing as she kept up with the quick tempo of the fiddler. She slid her foot sideways, then clicked her heels together, following the basic steps her mother had taught her as a young girl.

The music grew louder. How long had it been since she'd felt this free? Free to forget all the pain and loss she'd experienced the past two years and to simply live. This was a day for celebration. A day for new beginnings. Wasn't that what God was trying to tell her? Of course she'd never be able to forget Jarek. He'd always be a part of who she was — just like she'd never forget her parents. She couldn't change the past, but it was time to move on.

Give me a clean start, Lord.

She glanced at Adam, who still stood on the sidelines.

Is it too much to ask for a new start with Adam, as well?

Her feet kept time to the beat. She held her head high and let her arms move gracefully until the final note. The song ended too quickly. Trying to catch her breath, she moved away from the center of the floor.

Adam held up two glasses of punch in his hands. "I thought you might like something to drink."

"Thank you." Lidia took a sip, then placed her free hand on her heart, not sure if its rapid beat was from the exertion or Adam's nearness. "What did you think?"

"That I'm glad I didn't let you twist my arm into joining, though the dance was beautiful." His voice was barely above a whisper. "And so are you."

Lidia felt the heat in her cheeks rise. "It's a traditional dance that my people have done for centuries. It's a celebration of who we are."

He took a swallow of his drink. "You . . . you seem happier tonight."

"Being here today has confirmed who I am. It's reminded me that God can still give me happiness despite what's happened."

"Adam." Eric Johnson's voice broke into their conversation. "We could use your help over here for a moment."

Adam turned toward a group of men talking in the corner of the barn. "I'm sorry, Lidia. If you'll excuse me."

"Of course."

Lidia finished her punch and watched Adam join his father and several other men. The entire Johnson family had worked hard to finish the new barn for their neighbors. Sarah, Ruby, and Anna danced in circles along the side. Michaela, with little Daria clinging to her skirts, visited with several of the married women. It amazed Lidia that God had used this family to teach her so much about love, family, and true forgiveness.

"I didn't know you were such a talented dancer, Lidia."

"Silvia?" Lidia turned to her old acquaintance. She'd seen the young woman only a handful of times since her parents' death.

Silvia swayed to the music, letting the bottom of her dark green dress swish beneath her. "You looked as if you were enjoying yourself."

"I did. It's been quite a while since I had so much fun."

"That is a shame. I heard that you're working out at the Johnson farm now. A bit better, I suspect, though, than working at the mills."

Lidia stood up straight, determined to ignore the obvious jibe in Silvia's remarks. "I've always considered it a privilege to be able to provide for my brother and me."

"You are fortunate in that sense, I suppose." Silvia twirled the long sash that hung at her waist. "Adam Johnson is quite a good-looking man, isn't he? I know I certainly wouldn't mind working around him."

Lidia nearly choked. "Yes, I suppose he is. Good-looking, I mean."

"You suppose? Don't tell me you've never noticed."

Lidia sighed, wondering if there was a way to escape without being rude. She'd forgotten how annoying the woman could be. Still, she couldn't deny the obvious. "He's very good-looking."

"So you have noticed." Silvia smiled, and Lidia wondered what her motivation was with the personal questions. "I understand he even owns his own farm. A decent, hardworking man. You can't ask for much more than that, can you?"

"I suppose not."

"I saw him talking to you. Don't tell me you actually think he's interested you."

"I don't know. I . . ." The question caught her off guard.

"You are interested, though, aren't you? I saw the look you gave him right before he was called away." Silvia leaned forward. "Don't fool yourself, Lidia. If it weren't enough that you're an immigrant working out in his father's home, your brother murdered his brother —"

"That's none of your business."

"Maybe not, but no matter how hard you try, nothing can change the fact that you're not a native-born Yankee girl. Or that the people of this town will never completely accept you. You know how they think about girls who work outside the house. That's why my mother would never allow her girls to participate in such an undignified occupation."

"I'm an American. I'm Polish, and proud of both." A lantern dangled above her, casting eerie shadows across the barn wall. Lidia's stomach felt queasy despite her bold stance.

"Being an American is easy to talk about,

especially when you stand here surrounded by music from the motherland and more Polish food than an army could eat in a week. But you can't deny the fact that people look down on girls like you who work out on the farms. Manual labor is something no proper lady would ever be caught doing."

Lidia refused to back down. "There's nothing wrong with what I do, and besides, Adam's different."

"He's not different, Lidia. You just want him to be different. The reality is he'll settle with someone like me who comes from a well-to-do family and who would never lower her standards to be a servant."

Lidia held her breath as Silvia spun on her heels and walked away. The woman was incorrigible. Silvia held her head high as if she'd just done some noble deed by putting Lidia in her place.

Lidia pressed the fabric of her dress between her fingers. She couldn't argue with what Silvia had said. No Yankee or prosperous immigrant family would ever hire out their daughters to do housework at the local farms or in town. The jobs were given to impoverished girls like Lidia, most of whom were more than willing to help out their families by working outside the home.

Still, Lidia knew what the women in town thought. All girls wanted to be ladies, and it was degrading to be hired help.

Needing some fresh air and a chance to gather her thoughts, Lidia escaped through the large doors of the barn into the moonlight. Silvia had only confirmed something she'd known all along. The Johnson family had taken her in and treated her like family, but that wasn't enough. She would never be like Adam. She would always be the hired help. She'd wanted Adam's confession to change things between them, but was that even realistic? He'd tolerated the food and passed on the dancing, things that were so much a part of who she was. Would being born a Yankee have made him see her differently?

You were chosen to be who you are from the beginning, Lidia. You're Mine and I love you.

Lidia slowed her steps as she continued along the path toward the house. Words from her Savior filled her mind once again. They were words she wanted to believe, yet —

Lidia, I chose the exact time you would come into existence, and the exact place where you would live.

She stopped beside a fallen tree, stepping

188

over it so she could sit on its trunk and overlook the valley below. She clung to the words, knowing that they were true. Her heavenly Father loved her. What had the Psalmist written about her existence? God had created her, knit her together in her mother's womb, and every day ordained for her had been written down before she breathed her first breath.

The thought was too incredible for her to comprehend.

Music filtered into the night air . . . a million stars hung above her . . . a gentle breeze tugged at the base of her neck. . . . For too long, she'd lost her joy in the beauty of God's world and in His creation that surrounded her. Yet slowly, God was working to restore her joy.

No matter what happened around her — death, prejudice, injustice — she had to hold to one truth. Her existence wasn't a mistake. Men might live their lives full of hatred, but that would never change the fact that she'd been created in God's image. And He loved her.

She ran her fingers against the smooth bark of the fallen log. Silvia's words played in the back of her mind. She glanced up the hill and into the lighted barn. There was no denying that she'd seen the haughty expressions on people's faces when she'd gone into town. They might never consider her to be as good as they were, but she wasn't going to believe the lies anymore. What she'd told Silvia was true. She was an American and she was Polish. And she was proud to be both.

There was one other thing that was true, as well. If anything were to ever happen between she and Adam, he was going to have to accept her for who she was.

Adam scanned the crowd wondering where Lidia had gone. He felt as if he'd let her down. He'd never been much for parties and felt out of place tonight. He'd enjoyed working on the construction of the barn because he was good with his hands and knew he'd contributed significantly to the project. It was another story, though, when it came to dancing. He might as well try to swim across the Atlantic. He'd attempt that before trying to keep up with Lidia in one of the traditional Polish dances. And he'd never told her about what had really happened the day Samuel died. He knew now that nothing could ever happen between them if he didn't tell her the truth.

Grabbing another cup of punch, he took a sip, frustrated because he couldn't find her.

She'd looked so beautiful tonight, wearing the pale green dress he'd admired several times before. It might not have been as fancy as some of the other young girls', but its simplicity had only managed to set her apart. Her long hair had been pulled up, leaving tiny curls that framed her face and ran along the base of her hairline. He couldn't deny it anymore. He was in love with her.

He'd also seen something change within her tonight. He knew she still grieved over the loss of her brother. It was an emotion he understood all too well, but he hadn't missed the joy in her eyes as she'd stood beside her friends and danced. He loved to see her smile and wished that he had been the one to make her smile.

"Are you looking for someone?"

Adam turned around and tried to place the young woman who stood beside him.

"I'm Silvia Dolny. We met at church recently."

"I'm sorry. Of course."

"I only ask because you were looking a bit lost."

"Actually, I was looking for Lidia. Lidia Kowalski. Do you know her?"

"Of course." The young woman pushed a strand of her honey blond hair away from her cheek and smiled. "I've known Lidia for years."

"Have you seen her recently?"

She rested her fingers on his forearm. "I saw her slip out with someone a few minutes ago. Rufin, I think his name is. He's a tall redhead. You might have seen him tonight. He's quite a dancer."

"No. I don't think I've met him." Adam shook his head and tried to follow the young woman's implications. "I've been introduced to so many different people."

"Rumor has it they're engaged, or about to be anyway —"

Engaged?

Adam swallowed hard.

"I don't understand. How can Lidia be engaged?" It was a stupid question. He had no claims to her. Every time he'd been with her, he'd only managed to push her away. She certainly didn't owe him an explanation. He'd just thought . . . What had he thought? That saying he was sorry would erase all the pain that had piled up between them?

"Well, they're not technically, I suppose, but she just told me she was expecting Rufin to ask for her hand any time. Perhaps even tonight. It's the perfect setting, you know, so romantic. Apparently Rufin's been in love with her for years, but it's only been recently that he had the courage to tell her how he felt. Lidia's a sweet girl and all, but unfortunately she's been forced to work out —"

"I know. Lidia works for my parents."

"Well, of course you know then. I suppose they'll have to find someone to take her place before long, unless Rufin doesn't mind her working out. Some men don't mind their wives taking in menial jobs to help support the family, though personally —"

"If you'll excuse me." Adam ignored the shocked expression on her face and hurried to the other side of the barn.

He'd been a fool for so long. Pride had stopped him from forgiving Lidia's brother. It had caused him to turn against Lidia and her people. Pride had even stopped him from dancing with her tonight, afraid he'd make a fool out of himself. Now he was afraid that because of his pride, he might have lost her forever.

Fourteen

Adam strode out of the confines of the barn and stared into the darkness. A light breeze blew across his face but did little to erase the beads of sweat forming on his brow. He felt sick to his stomach. Surely there was nothing to the rumor that Lidia was engaged . . . or practically engaged to someone else. He should be the one courting her.

Lively music continued to play in the background while he scanned the path that meandered toward the Nowaks' darkened home. He looked for signs of Lidia and the redheaded Rufin, but there was little movement outside save the slight swaying of the trees that lined the walkway.

Shaking his head, he leaned against the side of the barn. Why should he be surprised if Lidia had given her heart to someone else? He didn't deserve her. She needed someone who wouldn't let her down the way he had. Someone who wouldn't make the same mistakes. Knowing he'd changed simply wasn't good enough.

"Adam?" His father stepped outside to join him, a bowl of stew in his hands. "I saw you leave. Trying to escape the celebrations?"

"You know I've never been much for parties. I needed a bit of fresh air." The spicy scent of the rich broth would have been tempting any other time, but at the moment, the thought of food soured his stomach.

His father took a bite of the thick stew. "Your leaving seems a pity with all those pretty girls inside, not to mention the great food."

Adam tried to laugh, but his voice rang hollow and empty. There was only one girl he cared about, and more than likely he'd lost her. He studied the other end of the yard where a number of tall trees were scattered over the terrain. If he ever did find this Rufin fellow, he had a few choice words he planned to say to the chap.

Adam's jaw tensed. "What do you know about a man named Rufin?"

"Rufin?" His father shook his head. "The name's not familiar. Who is he?"

"I don't know him personally, but I thought you might have seen him around the house. He's courting Lidia."

"What?" His father dropped his spoon into the bowl. "That's news to me. There haven't been any young men around our place looking for Lidia that I know of — except a certain son of mine."

Adam kicked the toe of his boot into the dirt. Why hadn't he done things properly from the beginning? He could have been the one courting Lidia. He could be the one holding her in his arms beneath the glow of the full moon. Instead he'd let her slip away.

"I just spoke to Silvia Dolny." Adam folded his arms across his chest. "She told me that Lidia was being courted by this Rufin. That he was going to ask her to marry him."

"Marcus Dolny's daughter?"

Adam shrugged. "I think so. I met her a few weeks ago at church."

"And are you sure she was telling the truth?"

Adam's brow rose in question. "What reason would she have to lie to me? I don't even know her."

"Has the thought ever crossed your mind that you're one of the area's most eligible bachelors, Adam Johnson?" His father cocked his head. "Don't tell me you haven't noticed the way Silvia and the other single women look at you."

He hadn't noticed anyone since he met Lidia.

"I could be wrong," his father continued, "but from what I've heard about Silvia, I wouldn't discount the idea that her comments regarding Lidia were nothing more than a ploy to get you to turn your affections away from Lidia — and onto her."

Adam frowned. "That's ridiculous."

"Maybe not. I just know that if I were in love with someone, I certainly wouldn't gamble my future on the words of a stranger."

His father was right.

Adam tugged on the collar of his shirt. "If you'll excuse me then, I'm going to find her."

His father nodded, and, not sure where else to go, Adam followed the path toward the house. Whether or not Rufin's intentions were valid didn't matter at the moment. He wasn't prepared to lose Lidia without a fight.

Adam stopped when he caught sight of her in the distance. She stood beneath the canopy of a large tree with Rufin, he presumed, who had his arms around her waist. Adam's fists clamped together at his side, and his teeth clenched together. Silvia had been right all along. Lidia was going to marry Rufin.

Lidia tried to push Rufin's hands off her waist; then she took a step backward. She never should have agreed to allow him to walk her toward the house to get her coat and bag. Lidia shoved against the man's broad chest with all her might, but the stocky man was too strong.

"Come on." His grip tightened around her waist. "I've seen the way you look at me. We could sneak down to the river and have a little fun tonight —"

Bile rose in her throat. "I have no intention of doing any such thing."

She could still hear the lively strains of the fiddle, but they were far enough away that she feared no one would hear her if she screamed. She'd been a fool to leave the celebrations alone. Rufin pulled her tighter, then pressed his mouth against hers. She jerked her head back and screamed.

Please, God . . .

Lidia closed her eyes and swung a fist upward hard.

"Ouch!"

"Adam?" Her eyes opened at the sound of his voice, and she sucked in her breath in horror.

Rufin's grip on her loosened.

With one hand nursing his jaw, Adam drew back his other fist and hit Rufin square in the chin before the thug had a chance to react.

Adam watched Rufin slide to the ground. The man was out cold and hopefully wouldn't awaken any time soon.

Rubbing his jaw, Adam turned to Lidia. "I never imagined you'd have such a solid swing."

"I can't believe I missed him and hit you instead." Lidia shook out her sore fingers, and from the look on her face Adam wasn't sure if she was going to laugh or cry. "How did you find me?"

"I was out looking for you and saw you struggling to push him away. I thought I could pull him off from behind. That's when I got in the way of your punch."

This time she chuckled. "I really am sorry. I didn't see you at all."

"It doesn't matter. He'll wake up and hopefully have learned a lesson. What were you doing out here with him?"

"I was talking to Silvia, and . . ." Lidia paused.

She'd been talking to Silvia? He didn't like where this was going.

"I needed some fresh air and decided to go to the house to get my coat. Rufin offered to walk with me. I've talked to him a few times at church, and he'd always seemed decent enough —"

"Until he decided to take advantage of you." Adam frowned.

"I was such a fool —"

"No, I've been the foolish one." He reached out to push back a strand of her hair that had fallen into her eyes. He wanted to pull her into an embrace and never let her go, but instead he tucked her arm into his and guided her back toward the festivities. They left the stirring Rufin to manage on his own.

"What do you mean you've been the foolish one?" She looked up at him as they headed back toward the barn, her eyes wide with question.

"Silvia had a talk with me, as well. She told me that Rufin had been calling on you."

"What?" Lidia stopped midstride. "That's ridiculous. I barely know the man."

"So there's no chance that you're engaged?" The question might be absurd, but he had to know for sure.

"Of course not. I wouldn't have let the man court me."

Adam let the music wash over him like a

soothing balm. He'd already waited too long to state his intentions.

He took a deep breath and gathered her hands into his. "I haven't been the same since I kissed you that night beneath the stars. I've made a mountain of mistakes, but I have to know one thing." He stopped, trying to gather his courage. "Is there any way you'd give me a second chance? Give us a second chance to see what might happen."

"I . . ." She pulled away from him.

"Lidia, please." He strode after her, wishing he could read her mind. "I can't deny any longer how I feel about you."

"It would never work, Adam." She looked straight ahead, avoiding his gaze. "I appreciate your saving me from Rufin, but we're two different people. I saw you in there tonight. You'll never be comfortable with who I am."

"That's not true."

"Isn't it?"

Surely he'd heard her wrong. He hadn't come this far to give up now.

"Lidia, stop for a moment. Please." He gently grasped her shoulder and turned her toward him. "If it's Samuel —"

"No." Lidia shook her head but this time didn't move away from him. "You don't understand, do you? It's not about Samuel anymore. It's about who I am, and how you see me."

"What do you mean?"

"Close your eyes and listen."

Not sure of why she wanted him to do it, he complied. The upbeat strains of a fiddle met his ears. Laughter and shouts radiated from the barn as people kept up with the traditional Polish folk dance. The smells of freshly cut wood and sawdust drifted through the night air, competing with the faint scent of her perfume.

He opened his eyes. The moonlight cast a ray of white light across her face and caught her pained reflection. He couldn't let things end between them this way.

She reached out and touched the edge of his sleeve before drawing her hand away, as if she was hesitant of what she was about to say. "This is who I am, Adam. I'll never be like your sisters or any other Yankee girl. People will always look down on me because of my heritage, and nothing you can say or do will ever change that."

"That's not true, and even if it is, it doesn't matter to me anymore."

"It matters to me." She took a step back. "I've spent my entire life trying to be someone else — an American. I've finally

202

realized that I don't need to be like them. I'm proud of who I am. God's been speaking to me lately. Reminding me that He chose me from the beginning —"

"And that He loves you for who you are." Adam finished her sentence with a half smile.

Lidia nodded. "Yes. How did you know?"

"God's been telling me the same thing lately."

"Really?" Her gaze penetrated his soul. It was more honest, searching, than anything he could think of. He could feel its pull.

Adam dug his nails into the palms of his hands. He'd almost decided not to tell her the truth. But there would never be a chance for anything to happen between them until he did. "There are things that took place the day Samuel died that I never told you. Things I've never told anyone."

"It's not too late. Tell me now."

Adam tugged on his ear lobe and forced himself to tell her. "I doubt if you heard about it at the time, but there was a series of events that happened right before my brother was killed. The sheriff had to handle more than the usual number of petty thefts, vandalism, and looting of stores. A Polish man named Artur was arrested for breaking into several of the stores in town, and most of us began to blame the incidents on the immigrants who had been flooding into town during the previous months."

He cleared his throat before continuing. "The day Samuel died, he and I had gone into town for supplies. On the boardwalk I overheard your brother saying something offensive to one of the shopkeepers. Jarek's accent made it obvious that he wasn't an American, and I made the comment to Samuel that . . . that it was high time the immigrants were sent back to Europe on the next cargo boat."

Adam winced at his own harsh words. How long had he prayed that he could erase the past? Yet it was something that could never be done.

Lidia's eyes darkened. "Tell me the rest of what happened."

"Your brother overheard what I said and pulled me into one of the side streets where he shoved me against the wall. Samuel had always been quick on his feet, and he tried to defend me. I pushed Jarek back, only to have Samuel throw the first punch. Before I knew it, things escalated out of control . . . and Samuel was dead."

Her eyes squeezed shut for a moment. "I'm sorry, Adam. I really am."

"Don't you see?" Adam's jaw tensed.

"Samuel's death was just as much my fault as it was your brother's. If I hadn't been filled with such bitterness for those coming into the area and spoken out of turn —"

"It's over, Adam."

He heard her words but didn't miss the pain in her voice. He knew what she was thinking. Would two lives have been spared if he'd had the sense to keep his bitter words to himself?

Lidia shook her head. "It's time you truly forgive yourself for what happened that day and go on with your life. You can't take back what you said any more than Jarek can erase what he did. It's time we all go on with our lives."

Adam took her hands in his. "If what happened is really in the past, and if you can totally forgive me, then let me court you properly. I can't let you go."

Lidia shook her head, and her eyes welled up with moisture. "I said I forgive you, and I meant it, but it's too late for us, Adam. There are simply too many obstacles standing between us. I saw how uncomfortable you were tonight. My people accept me for who I am. I'm finished pretending to be someone else."

For an instant, he saw the love he felt for her reflected in her eyes. He hadn't been wrong about her. She did care for him. If only he could get her to trust her heart.

He squeezed her hands. "Don't you see? I don't want you to be anyone else but Lidia Kowalski. Polish, American . . . Chinese . . . it doesn't matter to me. It's you I care about."

"I'm sorry, Adam." Lidia blinked back the tears and turned to run off into the night.

FIFTEEN

"Wait, Lidia."

Adam took half a dozen broad steps before he caught up with her. Reaching out his hand to grasp her shoulder, he turned her gently toward him. Tears streamed down her face as she looked into his eyes. "Adam, please . . ."

"Just tell me why. Give me one good reason why there's not a chance for us; then I promise I'll let you go and never bother you again."

She wiped away the tears from her eyes and shook her head. "You say that you care about me the way I am —"

"And you're not convinced?"

"Why should I be? You obviously despise my Polish culture. Besides, there are dozens of other girls who would jump at the chance to let you court them." She waved her hands in the air. "Dozens of girls who know how to serve a five-course meal or do fancy needlework like a proper lady."

"I'm not interested in any of that." He let his arms fall to his sides. "What is it? The differences between us can't be that great."

"Then you don't know me at all. Don't you see? I'll never be anything more than a common laborer, Adam. I have to work in order to provide for me and my brother, something no respectable Yankee girl would ever do."

She placed her hands firmly on her hips as she continued. "My mother tongue is Polish. I'm the daughter of a poor itinerate farmer who came to this country for a better life. I've had to work my entire life just to have enough to put food on the table. But I'm so much more than a poor immigrant from another country. I love dancing to traditional Polish songs and eating *bigos,* noodles, and cucumber beet soup. I love stories my babcia used to tell me. Tales of dragons, *Zlota Kaczka,* and other legends my people have passed on for generations."

Adam stifled a grin as she paused to take a deep breath. "Are you finished?"

She flashed him a look of impatience. "For now."

"I see a woman who loves books and poetry. Someone who can see beauty in a starry night and in the taste of maple syrup.

208

I see a woman who can work almost as hard as any man when she has to and who would give up everything to help a stranger. I see a woman who puts God first in her life and has finally discovered that He loves her exactly the way she is." Adam shook his head as he continued. "Just like you can't change who you are, I also can't change the fact that I was born in this country and only speak English. I can't help the fact that I feel more comfortable working my land than mixing at a social. But just because I can't dance and don't particularly like cucumber beet soup doesn't mean that you and I shouldn't take a chance together."

The corner of her mouth quivered upward. He took a step toward her and tilted her chin up with his forefinger. She was so close he could feel her warm breath against his skin, and it was all he could do to stop himself from leaning over and kissing her.

"You once told me that your people were no different from mine." He ran his finger across her jawline. "You said that while some immigrants make mistakes, all they wanted was what was best for their families — political and religious freedom and a place to call home. That's all I want, Lidia. Freedom, home, and a family. I see the way you look at me. Don't deny what your heart is telling you."

Lidia drew in a quick breath. Adam's words shook her to the core. She was afraid to hear what her heart was saying. Afraid that if she gave her heart away completely, he'd only end up breaking it. She'd spent her life dreaming that one day her own romantic champion would enter her life and sweep her away in one magical moment. Instead, she'd met a man whose past collided with hers . . . and still they had fallen in love.

She swallowed hard. When had love come into the picture? Looking up at him, she felt her chest tighten. The wind ruffled his hair, and she longed to run her fingers through the dark strands. His eyes pleaded with her. If she truly had fallen in love with Adam, then wasn't this a chance she needed to take? Her grandmother's tales of brave heroes and beautiful handmaidens all had happy endings. Perhaps God was offering her a happy ending, too.

Adam interrupted her thoughts as he took a step backward and bowed. "I was wondering, mademoiselle, if I might have this next dance?"

She caught his mesmerizing gaze, and her legs began to quiver. "You want to dance?"

"It's called a mazurra, I believe." Adam looked down at her and winked. "A traditional dance from Poland."

She tried not to laugh, but she couldn't help it. "It's called a *mazurka.*"

"Well, you've got to give a fine gentleman like myself credit for trying at least."

"I . . . I suppose you're right."

Lidia's heart pounded as she stepped into his arms. "You don't give up, do you?"

"On you? No."

A sense of unexpected joy washed over her. Like the night he first kissed her, it was as if this was where she'd always belonged.

She laughed as Adam tried to follow her lead. With her head held high, she let her hands move gracefully through the air. The fast tempo and syncopated rhythm left Adam struggling to keep up, but for the moment nothing seemed to matter except the fact that she was dancing with him beneath a moonlit sky.

He stepped on her foot, and she leaned forward to try to gain her balance. Grabbing her arm, he steadied her, then drew her toward him. His face hovered inches from hers.

She stopped dancing. "I . . ." Her mouth went dry and she couldn't speak.

Adam drew her hands toward his chest.

"There's something I've been wanting to ask you all evening."

"Yes?" This time she was ready for his question. This time she knew what she wanted more than anything else.

"Lidia Kowalski, may I have permission to court you?"

"I think today's the day." Sarah sat Indian-style on the picnic blanket and dangled a blade of grass between her fingers.

"The day for what?" Lidia rested against one of Adam's sugar maple trees and let the warm sun begin to lull her into dreamland.

"The day that Adam asks you to marry him."

Lidia's eyelids popped open. "Are you sure this time?"

"Well, not one hundred percent, of course, but pretty sure."

"Did he say something to you?"

"Not specifically."

Lidia closed her eyes again. "If you don't know for sure, then don't tell me."

"Why not?"

"Because you're making me nervous. On Easter you told me you were certain he was going to ask me, then again at his birthday celebration —"

"Just be patient. He'll ask."

Lidia frowned. She needed more than unsubstantiated feelings from Sarah. During her courtship with Adam he'd been the perfect gentleman, escorting her to church, accompanying her to socials, and even taking her out to dinner in town twice. But little had been said about their future. Silvia had dared to imply at one point that Adam had no intention of tying himself down to someone like her. While Lidia knew that the woman's words were meant to hurt, it was hard to ignore them all the same.

Sarah helped herself to a second slice of lemon cake out of the tin. "You have to admit that the very thought of Adam proposing is completely romantic."

Lidia didn't answer.

What *would* be romantic would be an actual ring on her finger and a wedding day set, though she'd never be so presumptuous as to say so to Adam. She'd dreamed about his asking her to marry him for weeks, and what their wedding would be like. While she didn't expect Adam to agree that the wedding be strictly Polish, she did want certain aspects of a traditional wedding to be incorporated into the day.

She envisioned the engagement when they would invite friends and family to witness the celebration of their commitment. Then on their wedding day his parents would give the traditional Bread and Salt Blessing at their house, and later there would be the Unveiling and Capping Ceremony that represented passage from being a young woman to a married woman. Drawing in a deep breath, Lidia could almost smell the tables of rich food that would be set out for everyone. Hunter's stew, dumplings, roasted meats with vegetables —

Lidia started as Adam's puppy jumped onto her lap and began licking her face. "Star!"

"I'll get him." Sarah stood and shooed the dog away before he caused any damage to their picnic lunch.

Lidia yawned as she shoved her half-empty plate to the edge of the blanket, surprised Star hadn't take off with her uneaten chicken leg. "If Adam doesn't come back soon, I'm going to end up sleeping through his proposal."

Sarah laughed. "If Ruby and Anna have their say, he won't even have time to propose to you today. He'll be too busy carrying them around the farm on his shoulders."

Five minutes later, Adam showed up with both girls. One on his shoulders and one holding onto his leg.

He's going to make such a good father. . . .

Ruby climbed down from Adam's shoulders as they approached the picnic blanket and plopped beside Lidia. "Are there any more of those sugary treats you made, Lidia?"

"I think so. Look in the basket."

When Sarah had convinced her stepmother to fix a picnic for the five of them, Lidia had volunteered to make the dessert. These special treats were one of her grandmother's favorites. Lidia's mother had taught her to make them soon after they'd arrived in America.

"They're called *chrusciki,*" Adam said, as he handed his sister a handful.

Ruby attempted to pronounce the name of the fried cookie, but ended up scrunching her lips together in frustration.

"My grandmother used to call them 'angel wings,' sweetie." Lidia reached out to smooth the back of Ruby's dark hair. "That should be a bit easier to say."

Ruby smiled. "That I can say."

Lidia nodded to Adam. "I'm impressed. Your Polish pronunciation is coming along quite nicely."

Adam let out a deep chuckle. "Considering I know about three words of the language."

Lidia laughed with him. All the doubts

she had ever had about Adam accepting her for who she was had vanished in the past few months. So much of the pain she'd experienced over her parents' and Jarek's deaths was beginning to heal. She still thought of them every day and made sure Koby remembered them, but the deep ache she'd carried inside her for so long was finally lessening.

Adam leaned close and gazed deep into her eyes. It always caused her stomach to do flips when he did that. "Don't you want to eat the rest of your lunch, Lidia? You've hardly eaten a thing."

"I'm fine, really." She smiled at him. Even if he didn't ask her to marry him today, the outing still would be perfect. She knew his sisters were important to him, and when they'd asked to spend the afternoon with him, he hadn't even hesitated. Lidia's presence, he'd told her, was icing on the cake.

"If you're finished, then, shall we go for a walk?"

"I'd love to." Lidia felt her pulse quicken.

"Don't worry about us," Sarah said. "We'll finish packing the picnic basket and load it into the wagon so Star can't get into it."

Adam reached down to help Lidia to her feet. His hand enclosed her fingers, sending tiny shivers up her arms. She tried to steady her nerves. Since the night Adam asked if he could court her, she'd known she wanted to marry him. But as ready as she was to get married, she knew they both needed time to get to know each other after all that had transpired between them.

The girls giggled and avoided Lidia's questioning gaze. Maybe Sarah really knew something and just hadn't been able to keep quiet. From the scheming looks on the three girls' faces, something was definitely afoot.

Briefly, Lidia touched the smooth texture of his shirt fabric before pulling her hand away. "What's going on?"

"Nothing." Adam shrugged a shoulder, then winked. "I've been doing a lot of thinking about the farm lately and need your opinion on something."

Lidia frowned. Talking about farm work wasn't exactly what she had in mind. She took his arm and let him lead her across the path toward the other side of the house. Summer had arrived, and the flowers that dotted the landscape were still in full bloom. The meadows and woodlands spread out before them in varying shades of green. A robin chirped, its cheerful sound mingling with the soft rustle of leaves from the afternoon breeze. With his arm around hers, Lidia smiled, wishing she could capture this perfect moment forever.

Adam pointed toward the south of his land. "I want to take some of the earnings I made from the syrup harvest to increase my herds of both cattle and horses by the end of the year. I know I'll have to start slow, but I want to make use of as much of the land as possible."

Lidia nodded. "I think that's a fine idea."

"One of my neighbors is moving and has promised me a fair deal on some of his livestock. I'm even thinking about dairy cows to produce my own cheese to sell."

"Cheese." Lidia tightened her lips, wishing she could be a bit more interested. It wasn't at all that she thought Adam's dreams were too big, or that he couldn't do it, but thanks to Sarah, she had marriage on her mind.

While she enjoyed listening to his dreams for the future, she didn't want to just hear about it, she wanted to be a part of it. They skirted the edge of the sugar bush, and Lidia couldn't help but feel the swell of pride within her. She had been a part of this year's harvest, working beside Adam once he'd recovered to ensure that the sap was collected and properly processed. It was what she wanted. To spend the rest of her life at his side.

218

Adam reached out and plucked a green leaf from one of the maples. "Next year I plan to harvest at least twice as much. . . ."

Adam's voice faded into the background as Lidia stared at a bird's-eye marking on the bark of one of the trees. Maybe she should say something to him, or at least attempt to draw him into a conversation regarding their future. She knew Silvia and her ugly words weren't true, but if Adam really loved her wouldn't he be thinking about *their* future instead of the future of his farm?

". . . I also want to —" Adam stopped and turned to face her. "Have you heard anything I said the past five minutes?"

"No — Yes." What could she say? That she was ready for him to ask for her hand in marriage?

"What is it?" A slight grin framed his expression as if he'd caught her with her hand in a penny jar.

"You've spoken about your plans for the house before. . . ." Lidia swallowed hard. "I was wondering about the house?"

"The house?"

"Yes." Lidia felt her confidence rise. She'd find a way to discover his intentions if it was the last thing she did. "I remember you saying at one time that you had plans for

219

the house."

He turned to look at the wooden structure. "The flooring needs to be replaced in at least one area, and I'd like to fix the front door. It creaks when you open it."

"Oh." She tried to hide the disappointment that flooded over her. He obviously didn't see the need of a new stove, or kitchen, or any other things a woman found essential.

"What's wrong?" he asked.

"Nothing."

Adam wrinkled his brow as if deep in thought. "There is one thing, though, that I could use your opinion on inside the house. Come."

The girls were nowhere to be seen as they made their way toward the house. Even Star's usual barks as he snapped at birds and butterflies had quieted.

"Where are the girls?" Lidia asked, trying to keep up with him as they took the stairs to the porch.

"Maybe they're in the house."

Adam opened the door, letting Lidia enter first. She stepped inside the living area then stopped abruptly. The room was full of people.

"Good afternoon, everyone. I didn't know . . ." Confused, Lidia turned to Adam.

There surrounding her was all of Adam's family. Mrs. Johnson with little Daria. Mr. Johnson with his arm around Koby. Mark and the three girls . . . even Star sat quietly on the hearth. Mrs. Gorski from church, who'd always been good enough to lend Lidia copies of her books, stood smiling beside her husband and two small children, as well as several other acquaintances from church.

Adam drew his arm around her. "Lidia, I wanted our engagement period . . . our *zareczyny* . . . to be what you've always dreamed it would be. I know it can't be the same without your parents and brother here, but I still wanted you to have a traditional Polish engagement."

Lidia's eyes filled with tears. "Our *engagement period?*"

Mrs. Gorski joined Adam's stepmother with a loaf of bread in her hands. "Your Adam here has been coming to see me to learn more about our Polish traditions and language. Today, if you say yes, Lidia" — laughter filled the room — "we want to ask God's blessing upon you. That you will always have bread beneath your hands and that your home will be filled with children and love."

Koby took a cautious step toward the

center of the room with a white cloth in his hands. "This is so that the two of you will always be bound together."

Lidia's eyes filled with tears. She couldn't believe Adam would do this for her. But he had, and this gift to her was one she'd never forget as long as she lived.

Adam turned toward her and took her hands. "Lidia Kowalski, there's nothing I want more than to spend the rest of my life with you. With these friends and family brought together as a witness of my love to you, I pledge to love and honor you always. Will you be my wife?"

She couldn't speak. She glanced around the room, tears streaming down her cheeks. Her gaze rested on each person, each smile filling her heart with emotion and an abundance of thankfulness.

Sarah caught her gaze and gave her a wry grin. "I promise this was a surprise to me, Lidia. Adam found out I'd been trying to discover when he was going to ask you to marry him, so he never told me."

Everyone laughed as Lidia turned back toward Adam.

"I'm sorry about the lecture on farming," he confessed. "It gave everyone a chance to sneak into the house —"

"And me a chance to squirm a bit?"

"I never said that, but you did deserve it, trying to find out." Adam smiled and squeezed her hands. "Will you marry me, Lidia?"

"Oh yes, Adam. Without a doubt, yes."

EPILOGUE

Ten months later

The day had finally arrived. Her wedding day.

Lidia fingered the ends of her braid and tried to calm the flutter of butterflies in her stomach. The night before, her customary single braid had been redone into two, symbolizing the step she was about to take in leaving behind her life alone to be joined with Adam in marriage.

She stood before the beveled mirror in Sarah's bedroom, making sure everything was perfect before going downstairs to meet Adam. The dark burgundy dress was by no means fancy, but in making it she'd added a few extra touches so it would be special for today. Three pearl buttons at the collar and lace around the edge of the sleeves and skirt for trim.

"Are you ready?" Rebecca held little Peter, she and Luke's nine-month-old boy, in one arm while adjusting the edge of Lidia's veil with the other. "You look beautiful."

Lidia offered her a weak smile. "And you're sure Adam will love the dress?"

She worked to steady her breathing at the wave of panic that hit her. Surely this was nothing more than a dream. The thought that Adam was right now waiting downstairs to take her as his bride was too wonderful to be true.

"The dress is perfect." Michaela stepped forward and drew her arm around Lidia's shoulder. "Besides, I have no doubt that he'll be looking at you and not your dress."

Lidia couldn't help but laugh out loud. She was surrounded by people who loved her, and she was about to become Mrs. Lidia Johnson.

See, I have turned your mourning into laughter. Your sorrow into joy.

Her heart swelled with praise at the reminder. While she desperately wished that her mother and father could be here to celebrate this day with her, God had taken away her sorrow and brought happiness back into her life.

"Come now." Rebecca opened the door to the room. "Everyone's waiting outside for the procession to the church. And your bridegroom is waiting downstairs."

Thanking God for His blessings, Lidia glanced up and nodded at Rebecca, who had become like a sister to her already. She was ready.

"I hope I'm next." Sarah's voice was full of longing as she followed Lidia into the narrow hallway.

"You're only fourteen." Rebecca nudged her sister gently. "It will happen one day. Then I'm sure you'll have an amazing and romantic story to recount to your grand-children."

Sarah blushed as they hurried toward the stairs of the Johnson family home to where everyone was waiting for them.

Lidia saw Adam the moment she began her descent of the staircase.

She drew in her breath as her gaze swept his face. His eyes reflected the smile on his lips. There was no doubt of his love for her. And no doubt in her own heart of her love for him.

Adam tugged on the bottom of his black suit jacket then stepped forward and took her hands as she reached the bottom. "You look . . . absolutely beautiful."

"Thank you. And you . . ." Lidia felt her cheeks flush.

She'd always thought him handsome, but today his touch left her breathless. He led her toward the front door of the house and out into the bright spring morning. "My father has prepared the traditional Polish blessing for us before we go to the church."

They moved to the front porch for the blessings, a part that was almost as important as the actual wedding ceremony. Everyone was dressed in their Sunday best. Many of the ladies had flowers pinned to their hats.

Mr. Johnson took their hands and pressed them together. "You look beautiful today, Lidia."

He turned to the group of people who stood waiting, and everyone hushed as he began his prayer. "O Lord, we come before You today to ask Your blessing on this couple. May their home enjoy an abundance of love, good health, and happiness. We know that life may be difficult at times, but may they learn to cope. To rely on each other, and most importantly, may they always remember to rely on You. Amen."

Lidia's eyes rimmed with tears.

Mr. Johnson turned and addressed the crowd with a wide grin on his face. "To the church, everyone. We've got a wedding to celebrate!"

Boisterous shouts burst from the crowd, and music began to play from the fiddler and double bass players, who stood in the back.

As everyone got into the wagons, Adam helped Lidia onto his buckboard. Sitting down, she breathed in the fresh spring air that was laced with the scent of fresh flowers. This ride to the church would be the last time she sat beside him as Lidia Kowalski.

The buggy bumped beneath them, but she was only aware of the joy in her heart. So much had happened since the day he'd rescued her from the rabid dog. She was amazed that God had brought them this far. And now they had the rest of their lives to enjoy together.

Adam wrapped his arm around her and pulled her close as they followed the dirt path. "There's something I forgot to ask Mrs. Gorski," Adam said.

"What's that?"

"Am I allowed to kiss the bride on the way to the church?"

"I don't know. I suppose if you wanted to badly enough."

"I do."

Lidia's heart raced in anticipation. "Then so be it."

Adam leaned forward and brushed her lips with promises of what was yet to come.

Floods of joy bubbled inside her. She pulled away briefly and looked into his eyes, knowing that she truly had found love in this New World.

ABOUT THE AUTHOR

Lisa Harris and her husband, Scott, along with their three children, live in northern South Africa, where they work as missionaries. When she's not spending time with her family, her ministry, or writing, she enjoys traveling, learning how to cook different ethnic foods, and going on game drives through the African bush with her husband and kids. Find more about her latest books at www.lisaharriswrites.com

The employees of Thorndike Press hope you have enjoyed this Large Print book. All our Thorndike, Wheeler, and Kennebec Large Print titles are designed for easy reading, and all our books are made to last. Other Thorndike Press Large Print books are available at your library, through selected bookstores, or directly from us.

For information about titles, please call:
  (800) 223-1244

or visit our Web site at:
  http://gale.cengage.com/thorndike

To share your comments, please write:
  Publisher
  Thorndike Press
  295 Kennedy Memorial Drive
  Waterville, ME 04901